Youry

Pío Baroja

Alpha Editions

This edition published in 2024

ISBN : 9789362997531

Design and Setting By
Alpha Editions
www.alphaedis.com
Email - info@alphaedis.com

As per information held with us this book is in Public Domain.
This book is a reproduction of an important historical work. Alpha Editions uses the best technology to reproduce historical work in the same manner it was first published to preserve its original nature. Any marks or number seen are left intentionally to preserve its true form.

INTRODUCTION

Pío Baroja is a product of the intellectual reign of terror that went on in Spain after the catastrophe of 1898. That catastrophe, of course, was anything but unforeseen. The national literature, for a good many years before the event, had been made dismal by the croaking of Iokanaans, and there was a definite *défaitiste* party among the *intelligentsia*. But among the people in general, if there was not optimism, there was at least a sort of resigned indifference, and so things went ahead in the old stupid Spanish way and the structure of society, despite a few gestures of liberalism, remained as it had been for generations. In Spain, of course, there is always a *Kulturkampf*, as there is in Italy, but during these years it was quiescent. The Church, in the shadow of the restored monarchy, gradually resumed its old privileges and its old pretensions. So on the political side. In Catalonia, where Spain keeps the strangest melting-pot in Europe and the old Iberian stock is almost extinct, there was a menacing seething, but elsewhere there was not much to chill the conservative spine. In the middle nineties, when the Socialist vote in Germany was already approaching the two million mark, and Belgium was rocked by great Socialist demonstrations, and the Socialist deputies in the French Chamber numbered fifty, and even England was beginning to toy gingerly with new schemes of social reform, by Bismarck out of Lassalle, the total strength of the Socialists of Spain was still not much above five thousand votes. In brief, the country seemed to be removed from the main currents of European thought. There was unrest, to be sure, but it was unrest that was largely inarticulate and that needed a new race of leaders to give it form and direction.

Then came the colossal shock of the American war and a sudden transvaluation of all the old values. Anti-clericalism got on its legs and Socialism got on its legs, and out of the two grew that great movement for the liberation of the common people, that determined and bitter struggle for a fair share in the fruits of human progress, which came to its melodramatic climax in the execution of Francisco Ferrer. Spain now began to go ahead very rapidly, if not in actual achievement, then at least in the examination and exchange of ideas, good and bad. Parties formed, split, blew up, revived and combined, each with its sure cure for all the sorrows of the land. Resignationism gave way to a harsh and searching questioning, and questioning to denunciation and demand for reform. The monarchy swayed this way and that, seeking to avoid both the peril of too much yielding and the worse peril of not yielding enough. The Church, on the defensive once more, prepared quickly for stormy weather and sent hurried calls to Rome for help. Nor was all this uproar on the political and practical side. Spanish letters, for years sunk into formalism, revived with the national spirit, and the new books in prose and verse began to deal vigorously with the here and now. Novelists, poets and essayists appeared who had never been heard of before—young men full of exciting ideas borrowed from foreign lands and even more exciting ideas of their own fashioning. The national literature, but lately so academic and remote from existence, was now furiously lively, challenging and provocative. The people found in it, not the old placid escape from life, but a new stimulation to arduous and ardent living. And out of the ruck of authors, eager, exigent, and the tremendous clash of nations, new and old, there finally emerged a prose based not upon rhetorical reminiscences, but responsive minutely to the necessities of the national life. The oratorical platitudes of Castelar and Cánovas del Castillo gave way to the discreet analyses of Azorín (José Martínez Ruiz) and José Ortega y Gasset, to the sober sentences of the Rector of the University of Salamanca, Miguel de Unamuno, writing with a restraint which is anything but traditionally Castilian, and to the journalistic impressionism of Ramiro de Maeztu, supple and cosmopolitan from long residence abroad. The poets now jettisoned the rotundities of the romantic and emotional schools of Zorrilla and Salvador Rueda, and substituted instead the precise, pictorial line of Rubén Darío, Juan Ramón Jiménez, and the brothers Machado, while the socialistic and republican propaganda which had invaded the theatre with Pérez Galdós, Joaquín Dicenta, and Angel Guimerá, bore fruit in the psychological drama of Benavente, the social comedies of Linares Rivas, and the atmospheric canvases which the Quinteros have painted of Andalusia.

In the novel, the transformation is noticeable at once in the rapid development of the pornographic tale, whose riches might bring a blush to the cheek of Boccaccio, and provide Poggio and Aretino with a complete review; but these are stories for the barrack, venturing only now and then upon the confines of respectability in the erotic romances of Zamacois and the late enormously popular Felipe Trigo. Few Spaniards who write today but have written novels. Yet the gesture of the grand style of Valera is palsied, except, perhaps, for the conservative Quixote, Ricardo León, a functionary in the Bank of Spain, while the idyllic method lingers fitfully in such gentle writers as José María Salaverría, after surviving the attacks of the northern realists under the lead of Pereda, in his novels of country life, and of the less vigorous Antonio de Trueba, and of Madrid vulgarians, headed by Mesonero Romanos and Coloma. The decadent novel, foreshadowed a few years since by Alejandro Sawa, has attained full maturity in Hoyos y Vinent, while the distinctive growth of the century is the novel of ideas, exact, penetrating, persistently suggestive in the larger sense, which does not hesitate to make demands upon the reader, and this is exemplified most distinctively, both temperamentally and intellectually, by Pío Baroja.

It would be difficult to find two men who, dealing with the same ideas, bring to them more antagonistic attitudes of mind than Baroja and Blasco Ibáñez. For all his appearance of modernism, Blasco really belongs to the generation before 1898. He is of the stock of Victor Hugo—a popular rhapsodist and intellectual swashbuckler, half artist and half mob orator—a man of florid and shallow certainties, violent enthusiasms, quack remedies, vast magnetism and address, and even vaster impudence—a fellow with plain touches of the charlatan. His first solid success at home was made with *La Barraca* in 1899— and it was a success a good deal more political than artistic; he was hailed for his frenzy far more than for his craft. Even outside of Spain his subsequent celebrity has tended to ground itself upon agreement with his politics, and not upon anything properly describable as a critical appreciation of his talents. Had *The Four Horsemen of the Apocalypse* been directed against France instead of in favour of France, it goes without saying that it would have come to the United States without the *imprimatur* of the American Embassy at Madrid, and that there would have appeared no sudden rage for the author among the generality of novel-readers. His intrinsic merits, in sober retrospect, seem very feeble. For all his concern with current questions, his accurate news instinct, he is fundamentally a romantic of the last century, with more than one plain touch of the downright operatic.

Baroja is a man of a very different sort. A novelist undoubtedly as skilful as Blasco and a good deal more profound, he lacks the quality of enthusiasm and thus makes a more restricted appeal. In place of gaudy certainties he offers disconcerting questionings; in place of a neat and well-rounded body of doctrine he puts forward a sort of generalized contra-doctrine. Blasco is almost the typical Socialist—iconoclastic, oratorical, sentimental, theatrical— a fervent advocate of all sorts of lofty causes, eagerly responsive to the shibboleths of the hour. Baroja is the analyst, the critic, almost the cynic. If he leans toward any definite doctrine at all, it is toward the doctrine that the essential ills of man are incurable, that all the remedies proposed are as bad as the disease, that it is almost a waste of time to bother about humanity in general. This agnostic attitude, of course, is very far from merely academic, monastic. Baroja, though his career has not been as dramatic as Blasco's, has at all events taken a hand in the life of his time and country and served his day in the trenches of the new enlightenment. He is anything but a theorist. But there is surely no little significance in his final retreat to his Basque hillside, there to seek peace above the turmoil. He is, one fancies, a bit disgusted and a bit despairing. But if it is despair, it is surely not the despair of one who has shirked the trial.

The present book, *Juventud, Egolatría*, was written at the height of the late war, and there is a preface to the original edition, omitted here, in which Baroja defends his concern with aesthetic and philosophical matters at such a time.

The apologia was quite gratuitous. A book on the war, though by the first novelist of present-day Spain, would probably have been as useless as all the other books on the war. That stupendous event will be far more soundly discussed by men who have not felt its harsh appeal to the emotions. Baroja, evading this grand enemy of all ideas, sat himself down to inspect and co-ordinate the ideas that had gradually come to growth in his mind before the bands began to bray. The result is a book that is interesting, not only as the frank talking aloud of one very unusual man, but also as a representation of what is going on in the heads of a great many other Spaniards. Blasco, it seems to me, is often less Spanish than French; Valencia, after all, is next door to Catalonia, and Catalonia is anything but Castilian. But Baroja, though he is also un-Castilian and even a bit anti-Castilian, is still a thorough Spaniard. He is more interested in a literary feud in Madrid than in a holocaust beyond the Pyrenees. He gets into his discussion of every problem a definitely Spanish flavour. He is unmistakably a Spaniard even when he is trying most rigorously to be unbiased and international. He thinks out everything in Spanish terms. In him, from first to last, one observes all the peculiar qualities of the Iberian mind—its disillusion, its patient weariness, its pervasive melancholy. Spain, I take it, is the most misunderstood of countries. The world cannot get over seeing it through the pink mist of *Carmen*, an astounding Gallic caricature, half flattery and half libel. The actual Spaniard is surely no such grand-opera Frenchman as the immortal toreador. I prescribe the treatment that cured me, for one, of mistaking him for an Iberian. That is, I prescribe a visit to Spain in carnival time.

Baroja, then, stands for the modern Spanish mind at its most enlightened. He is the Spaniard of education and worldly wisdom, detached from the mediaeval imbecilities of the old régime and yet aloof from the worse follies of the demagogues who now rage in the country. Vastly less picturesque than Blasco Ibáñez, he is nearer the normal Spaniard—the Spaniard who, in the long run, must erect a new structure of society upon the half archaic and half Utopian chaos now reigning in the peninsula. Thus his book, though it is addressed to Spaniards, should have a certain value for English-speaking readers. And so it is presented.

H. L. MENCKEN.

PROLOGUE

ON INTELLECTUAL LOVE

Only what is of the mind has value to the mind. Let us dedicate ourselves without compunction to reflecting a little upon the eternal themes of life and art. It is surely proper that an author should write of them.

I cultivate a love which is intellectual, and of a former epoch, besides a deafness to the present. I pour out my spirit continually into the eternal moulds without expecting that anything will result from it.

But now, instead of a novel, a few stray comments upon my life have come from my pen.

Like most of my books, this has appeared in my hands without being planned, and not at my bidding. I was asked to write an autobiographical sketch of ten or fifteen pages. Ten or fifteen pages seemed a great many to fill with the personal details of a life which is as insignificant as my own, and far too few for any adequate comment upon them. I did not know how to begin. To pick up the thread, I began drawing lines and arabesques. Then the pages grew in number and, like Faust's dog, my pile soon waxed big, and brought forth this work.

At times, perhaps, the warmth of the author's feeling may appear ill-advised to the reader; it may be that he will find his opinions ridiculous and beside the mark on every page. I have merely sought to sun my vanity and egotism, to bring them forth into the air, so that my aesthetic susceptibilities might not be completely smothered.

This book has been a work of mental hygiene.

EGOTISM

Egotism resembles cold drinks in summer; the more you take, the thirstier you get. It also distorts the vision, producing an hydropic effect, as has been noted by Calderón in his *Life is a Dream*.

An author always has before him a keyboard made up of a series of I's. The lyric and satiric writers play in the purely human octave; the critic plays in the bookman's octave; the historian in the octave of the investigator. When an author writes of himself, perforce he plays upon his own "I," which is not exactly that contained in the octave of the sentimentalist nor yet in that of the curious investigator. Undoubtedly at times it must be a most immodest "I," an "I" which discloses a name and a surname, an "I" which is positive and self-assertive, with the imperiousness of a Captain General's edict or a Civil Governor's decree.

I have always felt some delicacy in talking about myself, so that the impulsion to write these pages of necessity came from without.

As I am not generally interested when anybody communicates his likes and dislikes to me, I am of opinion that the other person most probably shares the same feelings when I communicate mine to him. However, a time has now arrived when it is of no consequence to me what the other person thinks.

In this matter of giving annoyance, a formula should be drawn up and accepted, after the manner of Robespierre: the liberty of annoying another begins where his liberty of annoying you leaves off.

I understand very well that there may be persons who believe that their lives are wholly exemplary, and who thus burn with ardour to talk about them. But I have not led an exemplary life to any such extent. I have not led a life that might be called pedagogic, because it is fitted to serve as a model, nor a life that might be called anti-pedagogic, because it would serve as a warning. Neither do I bring a fistful of truths in my hand, to scatter broadcast. What, then, have I to say? And why do I write about myself? Assuredly, to no useful purpose.

The owner of a house is sometimes asked:

"Is there anything much locked up in that room?"

"No, nothing but old rubbish," he replies promptly.

But one day the owner opens the room, and then he finds a great store of things which he had not remembered, all of them covered with dust; so he hauls them out and generally they prove to be of no service at all. This is precisely what I have done.

These pages, indeed, are a spontaneous exudation. But are they sincere? Absolutely sincere? It is not very probable. The moment we sit for a photographer, instinctively we dissemble and compose our features. When we talk about ourselves, we also dissemble.

In as short a book as this the author is able to play with his mask and to fix his expression. Throughout the work of an entire lifetime, however, which is of real value only when it is one long autobiography, deceit is impossible, because when the writer is least conscious of it, he reveals himself.

I

FUNDAMENTAL IDEAS

The Bad Man of Itzea

When I first came to live in this house at Vera del Bidasoa, I found that the children of the district had taken possession of the entryway and the garden, where they misbehaved generally. It was necessary to drive them away little by little, until they flew off like a flock of sparrows.

My family and I must have seemed somewhat peculiar to these children, for one day, when one little fellow caught sight of me, he took refuge in the portal of his house and cried out:

"Here comes the bad man of Itzea!"

And the bad man of Itzea was I.

Perhaps this child had heard from his sister, and his sister had heard from her mother, and her mother had heard from the sexton's wife, and the sexton's wife from the parish priest, that men who have little religion are very bad; perhaps this opinion did not derive from the priest, but from the president of the Daughters of Mary, or from the secretary of the Enthronization of the Sacred Heart of Jesus; perhaps some of them had read a little book by Father Ladrón de Guevara entitled, *Novelists, Good and Bad*, which was distributed in the village the day that I arrived, and which states that I am irreligious, a clerophobe, and quite shameless. Whether from one source or another, the important consideration to me was that there was a bad man in Itzea, and that that bad man was I.

To study and make clear the instincts, pride, and vanities of the bad man of Itzea is the purpose of this book.

HUMBLE AND A WANDERER

Some years ago, I cannot say just how many, probably twelve or fourteen, during the days when I led, or thought I led, a nomadic life, happening to be in San Sebastian, I went to visit the Museum with the painter Regoyos. After seeing everything, Soraluce, the director, indicated that I was expected to inscribe my name in the visitor's register, and after I had done so, he said:

"Place your titles beneath."

"Titles!" I exclaimed. "I have none."

"Then put down what you are. As you see, the others have done the same."

I looked at the book. True enough; there was one signature, So-and-So, and beneath, "Chief of Administration of the Third Class and Knight of Charles III"; another, Somebody Else, and beneath was written "Commander of the Battalion of Isabella the Catholic, with the Cross of Maria Cristina."

Then, perhaps slightly irritated at having neither titles nor honours (burning with an anarchistic and Christian rancour, as Nietzsche would have it), I jotted down a few casual words beneath my signature:

"Pío Baroja, a humble man and a wanderer."

Regoyos read them and burst out laughing.

"What an idea!" exclaimed the director of the Museum, as he closed the volume.

And there I remained a humble man and a wanderer, overshadowed by Chiefs
of Administration of all Classes, Commanders of all Branches of the
Service, Knights of all kinds of Crosses, rich men returned from
America, bankers, etc., etc.

Am I a humble man and a wanderer? Not a bit of it! There is more literary phantasy in the phrase than there is truth. Of humility I do not now, nor have I ever possessed more than a few rather Buddhistic fragments; nor am I a wanderer either, for making a few insignificant journeys does not authorize one to call oneself a wanderer. Just as I put myself down at that time as a humble man and a wanderer, so I might call myself today a proud and sedentary person. Perhaps both characterizations contain some degree of truth; and perhaps there is nothing in either.

When a man scrutinizes himself very closely, he arrives at a point where he does not know what is face and what is mask.

DOGMATOPHAGY

If I am questioned concerning my ideas on religion, I reply that I am an agnostic—I always like to be a little pedantic with philistines—now I shall add that, more than this, I am a dogmatophagist.

My first impulse in the presence of a dogma, whether it be political, moral, or religious, is to cast about for the best way to masticate, digest, and dispose of it.

The peril in an inordinate appetite for dogma lies in the probability of making too severe a drain upon the gastric juices, and so becoming dyspeptic for the rest of one's life.

In this respect, my inclination exceeds my prudence. I have an incurable dogmatophagy.

Ignoramus, Ignorabimus

Such are the words of the psychologist, DuBois-Reymond, in one of his well-known lectures. The agnostic attitude is the most seemly that it is possible to take. Nowadays, not only have all religious ideas been upset, but so too has everything which until now appeared most solid, most indivisible. Who has faith any longer in the atom? Who believes in the soul as a monad? Who believes in the objective validity of the senses?

The atom, unity of the spirit and of consciousness, the validity of perception, all these are under suspicion today. *Ignoramus, ignorabimus.*

NEVERTHELESS, WE CALL OURSELVES MATERIALISTS

Nevertheless, we call ourselves materialists. Yes; not because we believe that matter exists as we see it, but because in this way we may contradict the vain imaginings and all those sacred mysteries which begin so modestly, and always end by extracting the money from our pockets.

Materialism, as Lange has said, has proved itself the most fecund doctrine of science. Wilhelm Ostwald, in his *Victory of Scientific Materialism*, has defended the same thesis with respect to modern physics and chemistry.

At the present time we are regaled with the sight of learned friars laying aside for a moment their ancient tomes, and turning to dip into some manual of popular science, after which they go about and astonish simpletons by giving lectures.

The war horse of these gentlemen is the conception entertained by physicists at the present-day concerning matter, according to which it has substance in the precise degree that it is a manifestation of energy.

"If matter is scarcely real, then what is the validity of materialism?" shout the friars enthusiastically.

The argument smacks of the seminary and is absolutely worthless.

Materialism is more than a philosophical system: it is a scientific method, which will have nothing to do either with fantasies or with caprices.

The jubilation of these friars at the thought that matter may not exist, in truth and in fact is in direct opposition to their own theories. Because if matter does not exist, then what could God have created?

IN DEFENSE OF RELIGION

The great defender of religion is the lie. Lies are the most vital possession of man. Religion lives upon lies, and society maintains itself upon them, with its train of priests and soldiers—the one, moreover, as useless as the other. This great Maia of falsehood sustains all the sky borders in the theatre of life, and, when some fall, it lifts up others.

If there were a solvent for lies, what surprises would be in store for us! Nearly everybody who now appears to us to be upright, inflexible, and to hold his chest high, would be disclosed as a flaccid, weak person, presenting in reality a sorry spectacle.

Lies are much more stimulating than truth; they are also almost always more tonic and more healthy. I have come to this conclusion rather late in life. For utilitarian and practical ends, it is clearly our duty to cultivate falsehood, arbitrariness, and partial truths. Nevertheless, we do not do so. Can it be that, unconsciously, we have something of the heroic in us?

ARCH-EUROPEAN

I am a Basque, if not on all four sides, at least on three and a half. The remaining half, which is not Basque, is Lombard.

Four of my eight family names are Guipúzcoan, two of them are Navarrese, one Alavese, and the other Italian. I take it that family names are indicative of the countries where one's ancestors lived, and I take it also that there is great potency behind them, that the influence of each works upon the individual with a duly proportioned intensity. Assuming this to be the case, the resultant of the ancestral influences operative upon me would indicate that my geographical parallel lies somewhere between the Alps and the Pyrenees. Sometimes I am inclined to think that the Alps and the Pyrenees are all that is European in Europe. Beyond them I seem to see Asia; below them, Africa.

In the riparian Navarrese, as in the Catalans and the Genovese, one already notes the African; in the Gaul of central France, as well as in the Austrian, there is a suggestion of the Chinese.

Clutching the Pyrenees and grafted upon the Alps, I am conscious of being an Arch-European.

DIONYSIAN OR APOLLONIAN?

Formerly, when I believed that I was both humble and a wanderer, I was convinced that I was a Dionysian. I was impelled toward turbulence, the dynamic, the theatric. Naturally, I was an anarchist. Am I today? I believe I still am. In those days I used to enthuse about the future, and I hated the past.

Little by little, this turbulence has calmed down—perhaps it was never very great. Little by little I have come to realize that if following Dionysus induces the will to bound and leap, devotion to Apollo has a tendency to throw the mind back until it rests upon the harmony of eternal form. There is great attraction in both gods.

EPICURI DE GREGE PORCUM

I am also a swine of the herd of Epicurus; I, too, wax eloquent over this ancient philosopher, who conversed with his pupils in his garden. The very epithet of Horace, upon detaching himself from the Epicureans, "*Epicuri de grege porcum*," is full of charm.

All noble minds have hymned Epicurus. "Hail Epicurus, thou honour of Greece!" Lucretius exclaims in the third book of his poem.

"I have sought to avenge Epicurus, that truly holy philosopher, that divine genius," Lucian tells us in his *Alexander, or the False Prophet*. Lange, in his *History of Materialism*, sets down Epicurus as a disciple and imitator of Democritus.

I am not a man of sufficient classical culture to be able to form an authoritative opinion of the merits of Epicurus as a philosopher. All my knowledge of him, as well as of the other ancient philosophers, is derived from the book of Diogenes Laertius.

Concerning Epicurus, I have read Bayle's magnificent article in his *Historical and Critical Dictionary*, and Gassendi's work, *De Vita et Moribus Epicuri*. With this equipment, I have become one of the disciples of the master.

Scholars may say that I have no right to enrol myself as one of the disciples of Epicurus, but when I think of myself, spontaneously there comes to my mind the grotesque epithet which Horace applied to the Epicureans in his *Epistles*, a characterization which for my part I accept and regard as an honour: "Swine of the herd of Epicurus, *Epicuri de grege porcum*."

EVIL AND ROUSSEAU'S CHINAMAN

I do not believe in utter human depravity, nor have I any faith in great virtue, nor in the notion that the affairs of life may be removed beyond good and evil. We shall outgrow, we have already outgrown, the conception of sin, but we shall never pass beyond the idea of good and evil; that would be equivalent to skipping the cardinal points in geography. Nietzsche, an eminent poet and an extraordinary psychologist, convinced himself that we should be able to leap over good and evil with the help of a springboard of his manufacture.

Not with this springboard, nor with any other, shall we escape from the polar North and South of the moral life.

Nietzsche, a product of the fiercest pessimism, was at heart a good man, being in this respect the direct opposite of Rousseau, who, despite the fact that he is forever talking about virtue, about sensibility, the heart, and the sublimity of the soul, was in reality a low, sordid creature.

The philanthropist of Geneva shows the cloven hoof now and then. He asks: "If all that it were necessary for us to do in order to inherit the riches of a man whom we had never seen, of whom we had never even heard, and who lived in the furthermost confines of China, were to press a button and cause his death, what man living would not press that button?"

Rousseau is convinced that we should all press the button, and he is mistaken, because the majority of men who are civilized would do nothing of the kind. This, to my mind, is not to say that men are good; it is merely to say that Rousseau, in his enthusiasm for humanity, as well as in his aversion to it, is wide of the mark. The evil in man is not evil of this active sort, so theatrical, so self-interested; it is a passive, torpid evil which lies latent in the depths of the human animal, it is an evil which can scarcely be called evil.

THE ROOT OF DISINTERESTED EVIL

Tell a man that an intimate friend has met with a great misfortune. His first impulse is one of satisfaction. He himself is not aware of it clearly, he does not realize it; nevertheless, essentially his emotion is one of satisfaction. This man may afterward place his fortune, if he has one, at the disposition of his friend, yes, even his life; yet this will not prevent his first conscious reaction upon learning of the misfortune of his friend, from being one which, although confused, is nevertheless not far removed from pleasure. This feeling of disinterested malice may be observed in the relations between parents and children as well as in those between husbands and wives. At times it is not only disinterested, but counter-interested.

The lack of a name for this background of disinterested malice, which does exist, is due to the fact that psychology is not based so much upon phenomena as it is upon language.

According to our current standards, latent evil of this nature is neither of interest nor significance. Naturally, the judge takes account of nothing but deeds; to religion, which probes more deeply, the intent is of importance; to the psychologist, however, who attempts to penetrate still further, the elemental germinative processes of volition are of indispensable significance.

Whence this foundation of disinterested malice in man? Probably it is an ancestral legacy. Man is a wolf toward man, as Plautus observes, and the idea has been repeated by Hobbes.

In literature, it is almost idle to look for a presentation of this disinterested, this passive evil, because nothing but the conscious is literary. Shakespeare, in his *Othello*, a drama which has always appeared false and absurd to me, emphasizes the disinterested malice of Iago, imparting to him a character and mode of action which are beyond those of normal men; but then, in order to accredit him to the spectators, he adds also a motive, and represents him as being in love with Desdemona.

Victor Hugo, in *L'Homme qui Rit*, undertook to create a type after the manner of Iago, and invented Barkilphedro, who embodies disinterested yet active malice, which is the malice of the villain of melodrama.

But that other disinterested malice, which lurks in the sodden sediment of character, that malice which is disinterested and inactive, and not only incapable of drawing a dagger but even of writing an anonymous note, this no writer but Dostoievski has had the penetration to reveal. He has shown us at the same time mere inert goodness, lying passive in the soul, without ever serving as a basis for anything.

MUSIC AS A SEDATIVE

Music, the most social of the arts, and that undoubtedly which possesses the greatest future, presents enormous attractions to the bourgeoisie. In the first place, it obviates the necessity of conversation; it is not necessary to know whether your neighbor is a sceptic or a believer, a materialist or a spiritualist; no possible argument can arise concerning the meaning and metaphysics of life. Instead of war, there is peace. The music lover may argue, but his conceptions are entirely circumscribed by the music, and have no relation whatever either to philosophy or to politics as such. The wars are small wars, and spill no blood. A Wagnerite may be a freethinker or a Catholic, an anarchist or a conservative. Even painting, which is an art of miserable general ideas, is not so far removed from intelligence as is music. This explains why the Greeks were able to attain such heights in philosophy, and yet fell to such depths in music.

Music has an additional merit. It lulls to sleep the residuum of disinterested malice in the soul.

As a majority of the lovers of painting and sculpture are second-hand dealers and Jews in disguise, music lovers, for the most part, are a debased people, envious, embittered and supine.

CONCERNING WAGNER

I am one of those who do not understand music, yet I am not completely insensible to it. This does not prevent me, however, from entertaining a strong aversion to all music lovers, and especially to Wagnerites.

When Nietzsche, who apparently possessed a musical temperament, set Bizet up against Wagner, he confessed, of course, premeditated vindictiveness. "It is necessary to mediterraneanize music," declares the German psychologist. But how absurd! Music must confine itself to the geographical parallel where it was born; it is Mediterranean, Baltic, Alpine, Siberian. Nor is the contention valid that an air should always have a strongly marked rhythm, because, if this were the case, we should have nothing but dance music. Certainly, music was associated with the dance in the beginning, but a sufficient number of years have now elapsed to enable each of these arts to develop independently.

As regards Nietzsche's hostility to the theatocracy of Wagner, I share it fully. This business of substituting the theatre for the church, and teaching philosophy singing, seems ridiculous to me. I am also out of patience with the wooden dragons, swans, stage fire, thunder and lightning.

Although it may sound paradoxical, the fact is that all this scenery is in the way. I have seen King Lear in Paris, at the Theatre Antoine, where it was presented with very nearly perfect scenery. When the King and the fool roamed about the heath in the third act, amid thunder and lightning, everybody was gazing at the clouds in the flies and watching for the lightning, or listening to the whistling of the wind; no one paid any attention to what was said by the characters.

UNIVERSAL MUSICIANS

German music is undoubtedly the most universal music, especially that of Mozart and Beethoven. It seems as if there were fewer particles of their native soil imbedded in the works of these two masters than is common among their countrymen. They bring out in sharp relief the cultural internationalism of Germany.

Mozart is an epitome of the grace of the eighteenth century; he is at once delicate, joyous, serene, gallant, mischievous. He is a courtier of whatever country one will. Sometimes, when listening to his music, I ask myself: "Why is it that this, which must be of German origin, seems to be part of all of us, to have been designed for us all?"

Beethoven, too, like Mozart, is a man without a country. As the one manipulates his joyous, soft, serene rhythms, the other throbs and trembles with obscure meanings and pathetic, heartrending laments, the source of which lies hidden as at the bottom of some mine.

He is a Segismund who complains against the gods and against his fate in a tongue which knows no national accent. A day will come when the negroes of Timbuktu will listen to Mozart's and Beethoven's music and feel that it belongs to them, as truly as it ever did to the citizens of Munich or of Vienna.

THE FOLK SONG

The folk song lies at the opposite pole from universal music. It is music which smacks most of the soil whereon it has been produced. By its very nature it is intelligible at all times to all persons in the locality, if only because music is not an intellectual art; it deals in rhythms, it does not deal in ideas. But beyond the fact of its intelligibility, music possesses different attractions for different people. The folk song preserves to us the very savour of the country in which we were born; it recalls the air, the climate that we breathed and knew. When we hear it, it is as if all our ancestors should suddenly present themselves. I realize that my tastes may be barbaric, but if there could only be one kind of music, and I were obliged to choose between the universal and the local, my preference would be wholly for the latter, which is the popular music.

ON THE OPTIMISM OF EUNUCHS

In a text book designed for the edification of research workers—a specimen of peculiarly disagreeable tartuffery—the histologist, Ramón y Cajal, who, as a thinker, has always been an absolute mediocrity, explains what the young scholar should be, in the same way that the Constitution of 1812 made it clear what the ideal Spanish citizen should be.

So we know now the proper character of the young scholar. He must be calm, optimistic, serene … and all this with ten or twelve coppers in his pocket!

Some friends inform me that in the Institute for Public Education at Madrid, where an attempt is made to give due artistic orientation to the pupils, they have contrived an informal classification of the arts in the order of their importance; first comes painting; then, music; and, last, literature.

Considering carefully what may be the reasons for such a sequence, it would appear that the purpose must be to deprive the student of any occasion for becoming pessimistic. Certainly nobody will ever have his convictions upset by looking at ancient cloths daubed over with linseed oil, nor by the bum-ta-ra of music. But, to my mind, in a country like Spain, it is better that our young men should be dissatisfied than that they should go to the laboratory every day in immaculate blouses, chatter like proper young gentlemen about El Greco, Cezanne and the Ninth Symphony, and never have the brains to protest about anything. Back of all this correctness may be divined the optimism of eunuchs.

II

MYSELF, THE WRITER
TO MY READERS THIRTY YEARS HENCE

Among my books there are two distinct classes: Some I have written with more effort than pleasure, and others I have written with more pleasure than effort.

My readers apparently are not aware of this distinction, although it seems evident to me. Can it be that true feeling is of no value in a piece of literature, as some of the decadents have thought? Can it be that enthusiasm, weariness, loathing, distress and ennui never transpire through the pages of a book? Indubitably none of them transpire unless the reader enters into the spirit of the work. And, in general, the reader does not enter into the spirit of my books. I cherish a hope which, perhaps, may be chimerical and ridiculous, that the Spanish reader thirty or forty years hence, who takes up my books, whose sensibilities, it may be, have been a little less hardened into formalism than those of the reader of today, will both appreciate and dislike me more intelligently.

YOUTHFUL WRITINGS

As I turn over the pages of my books, now already growing old, I receive the impression that, like a somnambulist, I have frequently been walking close to the cornice of a roof, entirely unconsciously, but in imminent danger of falling off; again, it seems to me that I have been travelling paths beset with thorns, which have played havoc with my skin.

I have maintained myself rather clumsily for the most part, yet at times not without a certain degree of skill.

All my books are youthful books; they express turbulence; perhaps their youth is a youth which is lacking in force and vigour, but nevertheless, they are youthful books.

Among thorns and brambles there lies concealed a tiny Fountain of Youth in my soul. You may say that its waters are bitter and saline, instead of being crystalline and clear. And it is true. Yet the fountain flows on, and bubbles, and gurgles and splashes into foam. That is enough for me. I do not wish to dam it up, but to let the water run and remove itself. I have always felt kindly toward anything that removes itself.

THE BEGINNING AND END OF THE JOURNEY

I formerly considered myself a young man of protoplasmic capabilities, and I entertained very little enthusiasm for form until after I had talked with some Russians. Since then I have realized that I was more clean cut, more Latin, and a great deal older than I had supposed.

"I see that you belong to the *ancient régime*," a Frenchwoman remarked to me in Rome.

"I? Impossible!"

"Yes," she insisted. "You are a conversationalist. You are not an elegant, sprucely dressed abbé; you are an abbé who is cynical and ill-natured, who likes to fancy himself a savage amid the comfortable surroundings of the drawing-room."

The Frenchwoman's observation set me to thinking.

Can it be that I am hovering in the vicinity of Apollo's Temple without realizing it?

Possibly my literary life has been merely a journey from the Valley of Dionysus to the Temple of Apollo. Now somebody will tell me that art begins only on the bottom step of the Temple of Apollo. And it is true. But there is where I stop—on the bottom step.

MELLOWNESS AND THE CRITICAL SENSE

Whenever my artistic conscience reproaches me, I always think: If I were to undertake to write these books today, now that I am aware of their defects, I should never write them. Nevertheless, I continue to write others with the same old faults. Shall I ever attain that mellowness of soul in which all the vividness of impression remains, yet in which it has become possible to perfect the expression? I fear not. Most likely, when I reach the stage of refining the expression, I shall have nothing to say, and so remain silent.

SENSIBILITY

In my books, as in most that are modern, there is an indefinable resentment against life and against society.

Resentment against life is of far more ancient standing than resentment against society.

The former has always been a commonplace among philosophers.

Life is absurd, life is difficult of direction, life is a disease, the better part of the philosophers have told us.

When man turned his animosity against society, it became the fashion to exalt life. Life is good; man, naturally, is magnanimous, it was said. Society has made him bad.

I am convinced that life is neither good nor bad; it is like Nature, necessary. And society is neither good nor bad. It is bad for the man who is endowed with a sensibility which is excessive for his age; it is good for a man who finds himself in harmony with his surroundings.

A negro will walk naked through a forest in which every drop of water is impregnated with millions of paludal germs, which teems with insects, the bites of which produce malignant abcesses, and where the temperature reaches fifty degrees Centigrade in the shade.

A European, accustomed to the sheltered life of the city, when brought face to face with such a tropical climate, without means of protection, would die.

Man needs to be endowed with a sensibility which is proper to his epoch and his environment; if he has less, his life will be merely that of a child; if he has just the right measure, it will be the life of an adult; if he has more, he will be an invalid.

ON DEVOURING ONE'S OWN GOD

It is said that the philosopher Averroes was wont to remark: "What a sect these Christians are, who devour their own God!"

It would seem that this divine alimentation ought to make men themselves divine. But it does not; our theophagists are human—they are only too human, as Nietzsche would have it.

There can be no doubt but that the Southern European races are the most vivacious, the most energetic, as well as the toughest in the world. They have produced all the great conquerors. Christianity, when it found it necessary to overcome them, innoculated them with its Semitic virus, but this virus has not only failed to make them weaker, but, on the contrary, it has made them stronger. They appropriated what suited them in the Asiatic mentality, and proceeded to make a weapon of their religion. These cruel Levantine races, thanks only to Teutonic penetration, are at last submitting to a softening process, and they will become completely softened upon the establishment in Europe of the domination of the Slav.

Meanwhile they maintain their sway in their own countries.

"They are quite inoffensive," we are told.

Nonsense! They would burn Giordano Bruno as willingly now as they did in the old days.

There is a great deal of fire remaining in the hearts of our theophagists.

ANARCHISM

In an article appearing in *Hermes*, a magazine published in Bilbao, Salaverría assumes that I have been cured of my anarchism, and that I persist in a negative and anarchistic attitude in order to retain my literary clientele; which is not the fact. In the first place, I can scarcely be said to have a clientele; in the second place, a small following of conservatives is much more lucrative than a large one of anarchists. It is true that I am withdrawing myself from the festivals of Pan and the cult of Dionysus, but I am not substituting for them, either outwardly or inwardly, the worship of Yahveh or of Moloch. I have no liking for Semitic traditions—none and none whatever! I am not able, like Salaverría, to admire the rich simply because they are rich, nor people in high stations because they happen to occupy them.

Salaverría assumes that I have a secret admiration for grand society, generals, magistrates, wealthy gentlemen from America, and Argentines who shout out: "How perfectly splendid!" I have the same affection for these things that I have for the cows which clutter up the road in front of my house. I would not be Fouquier-Tinville to the former nor butcher to the latter; but my affection then has reached its limit. Even when I find something worthy of admiration, my inclination is toward the small. I prefer the Boboli Gardens to those of Versailles, and Venetian or Florentine history to that of India.

Great states, great captains, great kings, great gods, leave me cold. They are all for peoples who dwell on vast plains which are crossed by mighty rivers, for the Egyptians, for the Chinese, for the Hindus, for the Germans, for the French.

We Europeans who are of the region of the Pyrenees and the Alps, love small states, small rivers, and small gods, whom we may address familiarly.

Salaverría is also mistaken when he says that I am afraid of change. I am not afraid. My nature is to change. I am predisposed to develop, to move from here to there, to reverse my literary and political views if my feelings or my ideas alter. I avoid no reading except that which is dull; I shall never retreat from any performance except a vapid one, nor am I a partisan either of austerity or of consistency. Moreover, I am not a little dissatisfied with myself, and I would give a great deal to have the pleasure of turning completely about, if only to prove to myself that I am capable of a shift of attitude which is sincere.

NEW PATHS

Some months since three friends met together in an old-fashioned bookshop on the venerable Calle del Olivo—a writer, a printer, and myself.

"Fifteen years ago all three of us were anarchists," remarked the printer.

"What are we today?" I inquired.

"We are conservatives," replied the man who wrote. "What are you?"

"I believe that I have the same ideas I had then."

"You have not developed if that is so," retorted the writer with a show of scorn.

I should like to develop, but into what? How? Where am I to find the way?

When sitting beside the chimney, warming your feet by the fire as you watch the flames, it is easy to imagine that there may be novel walks to explore in the neighbourhood; but when you come to look at the map you find that there is nothing new in the whole countryside.

We are told that ambition means growth. It does not with me. Ortega y Gasset believes that I am a man who is constitutionally unbribable. I should not go so far as to say that, but I do say that I do not believe that I could be bribed in cold blood by the offer of material things. If Mephistopheles wishes to purchase my soul, he cannot do it with a decoration or with a title; but if he were to offer me sympathy, and be a little effusive while he is about it, adding then a touch of sentiment, I am convinced that he could get away with it quite easily.

LONGING FOR CHANGE

Just as the aim of politicians is to appear constant and consistent, artists and literary men aspire to change.

Would that the desire of one were as easy of attainment as that of the other!

To change! To develop! To acquire a second personality which shall be different from the first! This is given only to men of genius and to saints. Thus Caesar, Luther, and Saint Ignatius each lived two distinct lives; or, rather, perhaps, it was one life, with sides that were obverse and reverse.

The same thing occurs sometimes also among painters. The evolution of El Greco in painting upsets the whole theory of art.

There is no instance of a like transformation either in ancient or modern literature. Some such change has been imputed to Goethe, but I see nothing more in this author than a short preliminary period of exalted feeling, followed by a lifetime dominated by study and the intellect.

Among other writers there is not even the suggestion of change. Shakespeare is alike in all his works; Calderón and Cervantes are always the same, and this is equally true of our modern authors. The first pages of Dickens, of Tolstoi or of Zola could be inserted among the last, and nobody would be the wiser.

Even the erudite rhetorical poets, the Victor Hugos, the Gautiers, and our Spanish Zorrillas, never get outside of their own rhetoric.

BAROJA, YOU WILL NEVER AMOUNT TO ANYTHING

(*A Refrain*)

"Baroja does not amount to anything, and I presume that he will never amount to anything," Ortega y Gasset observes in the first issue of the *Spectator*.

I have a suspicion myself that I shall never amount to anything. Everybody who knows me has always thought the same.

When I first went to school in San Sebastian, at the age of four—and it has rained a great deal since that day—the teacher, Don León Sánchez y Calleja, who made a practice of thrashing us with a very stiff pointer (oh, these hallowed traditions of our ancestors!), looked me over and said:

"This boy will prove to be as sulky as his brother. He will never amount to anything."

I studied for a time in the Institute of Pamplona with Don Gregorio Pano, who taught us mathematics; and this old gentleman, who looked like the Commander in *Don Juan Tenorio*, with his frozen face and his white beard, remarked to me in his sepulchral voice:

"You are not going to be an engineer like your father. You will never amount to anything."

When I took therapeutics under Don Benito Hernando in San Carlos, Don Benito planted himself in front of me and said:

"That smile of yours, that little smile … it is impertinent. Don't you come to me with any of your satirical smiles. You will never amount to anything, unless it is negative and useless."

I shrugged my shoulders.

Women who have known me always tell me: "You will never amount to anything."

And a friend who was leaving for America volunteered:

"When I return in twenty or thirty years, I shall find all my acquaintances situated differently: one will have become rich, another will have ruined himself, this fellow will have entered the cabinet, that one will have been swallowed up in a small town; but you will be exactly what you are today, you will live the same life, and you will have just two pesetas in your pocket. That is as far as you will get."

The idea that I shall never amount to anything is now deeply rooted in my soul. It is evident that I shall never become a deputy, nor an academician, nor a Knight of Isabella the Catholic, nor a captain of industry, nor alderman, nor Member of the Council, nor a common cheat, nor shall I ever possess a good black suit.

And yet when a man has passed forty, when his belly begins to take on adipose tissue and he puffs out with ambition, he ought to be something, to sport a title, to wear a ribbon, to array himself in a black frock coat and a white waistcoat; but these ambitions are denied to me. The professors of my childhood and my youth rise up before my eyes like the ghost of Banquo, and proclaim: "Baroja, you will never amount to anything."

When I go down to the seashore, the waves lap my feet and murmur: "Baroja, you will never amount to anything." The wise owl that perches at night on our roof at Itzea calls to me: "Baroja, you will never amount to anything," and even the crows, winging their way across the sky, incessantly shout at me from above: "Baroja, you will never amount to anything."

And I am convinced that I never shall amount to anything.

THE PATRIOTISM OF DESIRE

I may not appear to be a very great patriot, but, nevertheless, I am. Yet I am unable to make my Spanish or Basque blood an exclusive criterion for judging the world. If I believe that a better orientation may be acquired by assuming an international point of view, I do not hold it improper to cease to feel, momentarily, as a Spaniard or a Basque.

In spite of this, a longing for the accomplishment of what shall be for the greatest good of my country, normally obsesses my mind, but I am wanting in the patriotism of lying.

I should like to have Spain the best place in the world, and the Basque country the best part of Spain.

The feeling is such a natural and common one that it seems scarcely worth while to explain it.

The climate of Touraine or of Tuscany, the Swiss lakes, the Rhine and its castles, whatever is best in Europe, I would root up, if I had my say, and set down here between the Pyrenees and the Straits of Gibraltar. At the same time, I should denationalize Shakespeare, Dickens, Tolstoi and Dostoievski, making them Spaniards. I should see that the best laws and the best customs were those of our country. But wholly apart from this patriotism of desire, lies the reality. What is to be gained by denying it? To my mind nothing is to be gained.

There are many to whom the only genuine patriotism is the patriotism of lying, which in fact is more of a matter of rhetoric than it is of feeling.

Our falsifying patriots are always engaged in furious combat with other equally falsifying internationalists.

"Nothing but what we have is of any account," cries one party.

"No, it is what the other fellow has," cries the other.

Patriotism is telling the truth as to one's country, in a sympathetic spirit which is guided and informed by a love of that which is best.

Now some one will say: "Your patriotism, then, is nothing but an extension of your ego; it is purely utilitarian."

Absolutely so. But how can there be any other kind of patriotism?

MY HOME LANDS

I have two little countries, which are my homes—the Basque provinces, and Castile; and by Castile I mean Old Castile. I have, further, two points of view from which I look out upon the world: one is my home on the Atlantic; the other is very like a home to me, on the Mediterranean.

All my literary inspirations spring either from the Basque provinces or from Castile. I could never write a Gallegan or a Catalan novel.

I could wish that my readers were all Basques and Castilians.

Other Spaniards interest me less. Spaniards who live in America, or Americans, do not interest me at all.

CRUELTY AND STUPIDITY

It appears from an article written by Azorín in connection with a book of mine, that, to my way of thinking, there are two enormities which are incredible and intolerable. They are cruelty and stupidity.

Civilized man has no choice but to despise these manifestations of primitive, brute existence.

We may be able to tolerate stupidity and lack of comprehension when they are simple and wholly natural, but what of an utter obtuseness of understanding which dresses itself up and becomes rhetorical? Can anything be more disagreeable?

When a fly devours the pollen greedily from the pyrethrum, which, as we know, will prove fatal to him, it becomes clear at once that flies have no more innate sagacity than men. When we listen to a conservative orator defending the past with salvos of rhetorical fireworks, we are overwhelmed by a realization of the complete odiousness of ornamental stupidity.

With cruelty it is much the same. The habits of the sphex surprise while bull fights disgust us. The more cruelty and stupidity are dressed up, the more hateful they become.

THE ANTERIOR IMAGE

I wrote an article once called, "The Spaniard Fails to Understand." While I do not say it was good, the idea had some truth in it. It is a fact that failure to understand is not exclusively a Spanish trait, but the failing is a human one which is more accentuated among peoples of backward culture, whose vitality is great.

Like a child the Spaniard carries an anterior image in his mind, to which he submits his perceptions. A child is able to recognize a man or a horse more easily in a toy than in a painting by Raphael or by Leonardo da Vinci, because the form of the toy adapts itself more readily to the anterior image which he has in his consciousness.

It is the same with the Spaniard. Here is one of the causes of his want of comprehension. One rejects what does not fit in with one's preconceived scheme of things.

I once rode to Valencia with two priests who were by no means unknown. One of them had been in the convent of Loyola at Azpeitia for four years. We talked about our respective homes; they eulogized the Valencian plain while I replied that I preferred the mountains. As we passed some bare, treeless hills such as abound near Chinchilla, one of them—the one, in fact, who had been at Loyola—remarked to me:

"This must remind you of your own country."

I was dumbfounded. How could he identify those arid, parched, glinting rocks with the Basque landscape, with the humid, green, shaded countryside of Azpeitia? It was easy to see that the anterior image of a landscape existing in the mind of that priest, provided only the general idea of a mountain, and that he was unable to distinguish, as I was, between a green mountain overgrown with turf and trees, and an arid hillside of dry rocks.

An hypothesis explaining the formation of visual ideas has been formulated by Wundt, which he calls the hypothesis of projection. It attributes to the retina an innate power of referring its impressions outward along straight lines, in directions which are determined.

According to Müller, who has adopted this hypothesis, what we perceive is our own retina under the category of space, and the size of the retinal image is the original unit of measurement applied by us to exterior objects.

The Spaniard like a child, will have to amplify his retinal image, if he is ever to amount to anything. He will have to amplify it, and, no doubt, complicate it also.

THE TRAGI-COMEDY OF SEX

It is very difficult to approach the sex question and to treat it at once in a clear and dignified manner. And yet, who can deny that it furnishes the key to the solution of many of the enigmas and obscurities of psychology?

Who can question that sex is one of the bases of temperament?

Nevertheless, the subject may be discussed permissibly in scientific and very general terms, as by Professor Freud. What is unpardonable is any attempt to bring it down to the sphere of the practical and concrete.

I am convinced that the repercussion of the sexual life is felt through all the phenomena of consciousness.

According to Freud, an unsatisfied desire produces a series of obscure movements in consciousness which eat at the soul as electricity is generated in a storage battery, and this accumulation of psychic energy must needs produce a disturbance in the nervous system.

Such nervous disturbances, which are of sexual origin, produced by the strangulation of desires, shape our mentality.

What is the proper conduct for a man during the critical years between the ages of fourteen and twenty-three? He should be chaste, the priests will say, shutting their eyes with an hypocritical air. He can marry afterwards and become a father.

A man who can be chaste without discomfort between fourteen and twenty-three, is endowed with a most unusual temperament. And it is one which is not very common at present. As a matter of fact, young men are not chaste, and cannot be.

Society, as it is well aware of this, opens a little loophole to sexuality, which is free from social embarrassment—the loophole of prostitution.

As the bee-hive has its workers, society has its prostitutes.

After a few years of sexual life without the walls, passed in the surrounding moats of prostitution, the normal man is prepared for marriage, with its submission to social forms and to standards which are clearly absurd.

There is no possibility of escaping this dilemma which has been decreed by society.

The alternative is perversion or surrender.

To a man of means, who has money to spend, surrender is not very difficult; he has but to follow the formula. Prostitution among the upper classes does not offend the eye, and it reveals none of the sores which deface prostitution as it is practised among the poor. Marriage, too, does not sit heavily upon the rich. With the poor, however, shame and surrender walk hand in hand.

To practise the baser forms of prostitution is to elbow all that is most vile in society, and to sink to its level oneself. Then, to marry afterwards without adequate means, is a continual act of self-abasement. It is to be unable to maintain one's convictions, it is to be compelled to fawn upon one's superiors, and this is more true in Spain than it is elsewhere, as everything here must be obtained through personal influence.

Suppose one does not submit? If you do not submit you are lost. You are condemned irretrievably to perversions, to debility, to hysteria.

You will find yourself slinking about the other sex like a famished wolf, you will live obsessed by lewd ideas, your mind will solace itself with swindles and cheats wherewith to provide a solution of the riddle of existence, you will become the mangy sheep that the shepherd sets apart from the flock.

Ever since early youth, I have been clearly conscious of this dilemma, and I have determined and said: "No; I choose the abnormal—give me hysteria, but submission, never!"

So derangement and distortion have come to my mind.

If I could have followed my inclinations freely during those fruitful years between fifteen and twenty-five, I should have been a serene person, a little sensual, perhaps, and perhaps a little cynical, but I should certainly not have become violent.

The morality of our social system has disturbed and upset me.

For this reason I hate it cordially, and I vent upon it in full measure, as best I may, all the spleen I have to give.

I like at times to disguise this poison under a covering of art.

THE VEILS OF THE SEXUAL LIFE

I am unable to feel any spontaneous enthusiasm for fecundity such as that which Zola sings. Moreover, I regard the whole pose as a superstition. I may be a member of an exhausted race,—that is quite possible,—but between the devotion to our species which is professed by these would-be re-peoplers of countries, and the purely selfish preoccupation of the Malthusians, my sympathies are all with the latter. I see nothing beyond the individual in this sex question—beyond the individual who finds himself inhibited by sexual morality.

This question must be faced some day and cleared up, it must be seen divested of all mystery, of all veils, of all deceit. As the hygiene of nutrition has been studied openly, in broad daylight, so it must be with sex hygiene.

As a matter of fact, the notion of sin, then, that of honour, and, finally, dread of syphilis and other sexual diseases, rest like a cloud on the sexual life, and they are jumbled together with all manner of fantastic and literary fictions.

Obviously, rigid sexual morality is for the most part nothing more than the practice of economy in disguise. Let us face this whole problem frankly. A man has no right to let his life slip by to gratify fools' follies. We must have regard to what is, with Stendhal. It will be argued of course that these veils, these subterfuges of the sexual life, are necessary. No doubt they are to society, but they are not to the individual. There are those who believe that the interests of the individual and of society are one, but we, who are defenders of the individual as against the State, do not think so.

A LITTLE TALK

Myself: I often think I should have been happier if I had been impotent.

My Hearers: How can you say such a terrible thing?

Myself: Why not? To a man like me, sex is nothing but a source of misery, shame and cheap hypocrisy, as it is to most of us who are obliged to get on without sufficient means under this civilization of ours. Now you know why I think that I should have been better off if I had been impotent.

UPON THE SUPPOSED MORALITY OF MARRIAGE

Single life is said to be selfish and detestable. Certainly it is immoral. But what of marriage? Is it as moral as it is painted?

I am one who doubts it.

Marriage, like all other social institutions of consequence, is surrounded by a whole series of common assumptions that cry out to be cleared up.

There is a pompous and solemn side to marriage, and there is a private museum side.

Marriage poses as an harmonious general concord in which religion, society, and nature join.

But is it anything of the kind? It would appear to be doubtful. If the sole purpose of marriage is to rear children, a man ought to live with a woman only until she becomes pregnant, and, after that moment, he ought not to touch her. But here begins the second part. The woman bears a baby; the baby is nourished by the mother's milk. The man has no right to co-habit with his wife during this period either, because it will be at the risk of depriving the child of its natural source of nutriment.

In consequence, a man must either co-habit with his wife once in two years, or else there will be some default in the marriage.

What is he to do? What is the moral course? Remember that three factors have combined to impose the marriage. One, the most far-reaching today, is economic; another, which is also extremely important, is social, and the third, now rapidly losing its hold, but still not without influence, is religious. The three forces together attempt to mould nature to their will.

Economic pressure and the high cost of living make against the having of children. They encourage default.

"How are we to have all these children?" the married couple asks. "How can we feed and educate them?"

Social pressure also tends in the same direction. Religious morality, however, still persists in its idea of sin, although the potency of this sanction is daily becoming less, even to the clerical eye.

If nature had a vote, it would surely be cast in favour of polygamy. Man is forever sexual, and in equal degree, until the verge of decrepitude. Woman passes through the stages of fecundation, pregnancy, and lactation.

There can be no doubt but that the most convenient, the most logical and the most moral system of sexual intercourse, naturally, is polygamy.

But the economic subdues the natural. Who proposes to have five wives when he cannot feed one?

Society has made man an exclusively social product, and set him apart from nature.

What can the husband and wife do, especially when they are poor? Must they overload themselves with children, and then deliver them up to poverty and neglect because God has given them, or shall they limit their number?

If my opinion is asked, I advise a limit—although it may be artificial and immoral.

Marriage presents us with this simple choice: we may either elect the slow, filthy death of the indigent workingman, of the carabineer who lives in a shack which teems with children, or else the clean life of the French, who limit their offspring.

The middle class everywhere today is accepting the latter alternative. Marriage is stripping off its morality in the bushes, and it is well that it should do so.

THE SOVEREIGN CROWD

A strong man may either dominate and subdue the sovereign crowd when he confronts it, as he would a wild beast, or he may breathe his thoughts and ideas into it, which is only another form of domination.

As I am not strong enough to do either, I shun the sovereign masses, so as not to become too keenly conscious of their collective bestiality and ill temper.

THE REMEDY

Every man fancies that he has something of the doctor in him, and considers himself competent to advise some sort of a cure, so I come now with a remedy for the evils of life. My remedy is constant action. It is a cure as old as the world, and it may be as useful as any other, and doubtless it is as futile as all the rest. As a matter of fact, it is no remedy at all.

The springs of action lie all within ourselves, and they derive from the vigour and health which we have inherited from our fathers. The man who possesses them may draw on them whenever he will, but the man who is without them can never acquire them, no matter how widely he may seek.

III

THE EXTRARADIUS

The extraradius of a writer may be said to be made up of his literary opinions and inclinations. I wish to expose the literary cell from the nucleus out and to unfold it, instead of proceeding in from the covering.

The term may seem pedantic and histological, but it has the attraction to my mind of a reminiscence of student days.

RHETORIC AND ANTI-RHETORIC

If I were to formulate my opinions upon style, I should say: "Imitations of other men's styles are bad, but a man's own style is good."

There is a store of common literary finery, almost all of which is in constant use and has become familiar.

When a writer lays hands on any of this finery spontaneously, he makes it his own, and the familiar flower blossoms as it does in Nature.

When an author's inspiration does not proceed from within out, but rather from without in, then he becomes at once a bad rhetorician.

I am one of those writers who employ the least possible amount of this common store of rhetoric. There are various reasons for my being anti-rhetorical. In the first place I do not believe that the pages of a bad writer can be improved by following general rules; if they do gain in one respect, they lose inevitably in another.

So much for one reason; but I have others.

Languages display a tendency to follow established forms. Thus Spanish tends toward Castilian. But why should I, a Basque, who never hears Castilian spoken in my daily life in the accents of Avila or of Toledo, endeavour to imitate it? Why should I cease to be a Basque in order to appear Castilian, when I am not? Not that I cherish sectional pride, far from it; but every man should be what he is, and if he can be content with what he is, let him be held fortunate.

For this reason, among others, I reject Castilian turns and idioms when they suggest themselves to my mind. Thus if it occurs to me to write something that is distinctively Castilian, I cast about for a phrase by means of which I may express myself in what to me is a more natural way, without suggestion of our traditional literature.

On the other hand, if the pure rhetoricians, of the national school, who are *castizo*—the Mariano de Cavias, the Ricardo Leóns—should happen to write something simply, logically and with modern directness, they would cast about immediately for a roundabout way of saying it, which might appear elaborate and out of date.

THE RHYTHM OF STYLE

There are persons who imagine that I am ignorant of the three or four elementary rules of good writing, which everybody knows, while others believe that I am unacquainted with syntax. Señor Bonilla y San Martín has conducted a search through my books for deficiencies, and has discovered that in one place I write a sentence in such and such fashion, and that in another I write something else in another, while in a third I compound a certain word falsely.

With respect to the general subject of structural usage which he raises, it would be easy to cite ample precedent among our classic authors; with respect to the word *misticidad* occurring in one of my books, I have put it into the mouth of a foreigner. The faults brought to light by Señor Bonilla are not very serious. But what of it? Suppose they were?

An intelligent friend once said to me:

"I don't know what is lacking in your style; I find it acrid." I feel that this criticism is the most apt that has yet been made.

My difficulty in writing Castilian does not arise from any deficiency in grammar nor any want of syntax. I fail in measure, in rhythm of style, and this shocks those who open my books for the first time. They note that there is something about them that does not sound right, which is due to the fact that there is a manner of respiration in them, a system of pauses, which is not traditionally Castilian.

I should insist upon the point at greater length, were it not that the subject of style is cluttered up with such a mass of preconceptions, that it would be necessary to redefine our terminology, and then, after all, perhaps we should not understand one another. Men have an idea that they are thinking when they operate the mechanism of language which they have at command. When somebody makes the joints of language creak, they say: "He does not know how to manage it." Certainly he does know how to manage it. Anybody can manage a platitude. The truth is simply this: the individual writer endeavours to make of language a cloak to fit his form, while, contrarywise, the purists attempt to mould their bodies till they fit the cloak.

RHETORIC OF THE MINOR KEY

Persons to whom my style is not entirely distasteful, sometimes ask:

"Why use the short sentence when it deprives the period of eloquence and rotundity?"

"Because I do not desire eloquence or rotundity," I reply. "Furthermore, I avoid them." The vast majority of Spanish purists are convinced that the only possible rhetoric is the rhetoric of the major key. This, for example, is the rhetoric of Castelar and Costa, the rhetoric which Ricardo León and Salvador Rueda manipulate today, as it has been inherited from the Romans. Its purpose is to impart solemnity to everything, to that which already has it by right of nature, and to that which has it not. This rhetoric of the major key marches with stately, academic tread. At great, historic moments, no doubt it is very well, but in the long run, in incessant parade, it is one of the most deadly soporifics in literature; it destroys variety, it is fatal to subtlety, to nice transitions, to detail, and it throws the uniformity of the copybook over everything.

On the other hand, the rhetoric of the minor key, which seems poor at first blush, soon reveals itself to be more attractive. It moves with a livelier, more life-like rhythm; it is less bombastic. This rhetoric implies continence and basic economy of effort; it is like an agile man, lightly clothed and free of motion.

To the extent of my ability I always avoid the rhetoric of the major key, which is assumed as the only proper style, the very moment that one sits down to write Castilian. I should like, of course, to rise to the heights of solemnity now and then, but very seldom.

"Then what you seek," I am told, "is a familiar style like that of Mesonero Romanos, Trueba and Pereda?"

No, I am not attracted by that either.

The familiar, rude, vulgar manner reminds me of a worthy bourgeois family at the dinner table. There sits the husband in his shirt sleeves, while the wife's hair is at loose ends and she is dirty besides, and all the children are in rags.

I take it that one may be simple and sincere without either affectation or vulgarity. It is well to be a little neutral, perhaps, a little grey for the most part, so that upon occasion the more delicate hues may stand out clearly, while a rhythm may be employed to advantage which is in harmony with actual life, which is light and varied, and innocent of striving after solemnity.

A modern poet, in my opinion, has illustrated this rhetoric of the minor key to perfection.

He is Paul Verlaine.

A style like Verlaine's, which is non-sequent, macerated, free, is indispensable to any mastery of the rhetoric of the minor key. This, to me, has always been my literary ideal.

THE VALUE OF MY IDEAS

From time to time, my friend Azorín attempts to analyse my ideas. I do not pretend to be in the secret of the scales, as such an assumption upon my part would be ridiculous. As the pilot takes advantage of a favourable wind, and if it does not blow, of one that is unfavourable, I do the same. The meteorologist is able to tell with mathematical accuracy in his laboratory, after a glance at his instruments, not only the direction of the prevailing wind, but the atmospheric pressure and the degree of humidity as well. I am able only, however, to say with the pilot: "I sail this way," and then make head as best I may.

GENIUS AND ADMIRATION

I have no faith in the contention of the Lombrosians that genius is akin to insanity, neither do I think that genius is an infinite capacity for taking pains. Lombroso, for that matter, is as old-fashioned today as a hoop skirt.

Genius partakes of the miraculous. If some one should tell me that a stick had been transformed into a snake by a miracle, naturally I should not believe it; but if I should be asked whether there was not something miraculous in the very existence of a stick or of a snake, I should be constrained to acknowledge the miracle.

When I read the lives of the philosophers in Diogenes Laertius, I arrive at the conclusion that Epicurus, Zeno, Diogenes, Protagoras and the others were nothing more than men who had common sense. Clearly, as a corollary, I am obliged to conclude that the people we meet nowadays upon the street, whether they wear gowns, uniforms or blouses, are mere animals masquerading in human shape.

Contradicting the assumption that the great men of antiquity were only ordinary normal beings, we must concede the fact that most extraordinary conditions must have existed and, indeed, have been pre-exquisite, before a Greece could have arisen in antiquity, or an Athens in Greece, or a man such as Plato in Athens.

By very nature, the sources of admiration are as mysterious to my mind as the roots of genius. Do we admire what we understand, or what we do not understand? Admiration is of two kinds, of which the more common proceeds from wonder at something which we do not understand. There is, however, an admiration which goes with understanding.

Edgar Poe composed several stories, of which *The Goldbug* is one, in which an impenetrable enigma is first presented, to be solved afterwards as by a talisman; but, then, a lesson in cryptography ensues, wherein the talisman is explained away, and the miraculous gives place to the reasoning faculties of a mind of unusual power.

He has done something very similar in his poem, *The Raven*, where the poem is followed by an analysis of its gestation, which is called *The Philosophy of Composition*. Would it be more remarkable to write *The Raven* by inspiration, or to write it through conscious skill? To find the hidden treasure through the talisman of *The Goldbug*, or through the possession of analytical faculties such as those of the protagonist of Poe's tale?

Much consideration will lead to the conclusion that one process is as marvellous as the other.

It may be said that there is nothing miraculous in nature, and it may be said that it is all miraculous.

MY LITERARY AND ARTISTIC INCLINATIONS

Generally speaking, I neither understand old books very well, nor do I care for them—I have been able to read only Shakespeare, and perhaps one or two others, with the interest with which I approach modern writers.

It has sometimes seemed to me that the unreadableness of the older authors might be made the foundation of a philosophic system. Yet I have met with some surprises.

One was that I enjoyed the *Odyssey*.

"Am I a hypocrite?" I asked myself.

I do not find old painters to be as incompatible as old authors. On the contrary, my experience has been that they are the reverse. I greatly prefer a canvas by Botticelli, Mantegna, El Greco or Velázquez to a modern picture.

The only famous painter of the past for whom I have entertained an antipathy, is Raphael; yet, when I was in Rome and saw the frescos in the Vatican, I was obliged again to ask myself if my attitude was a pose, because they struck me frankly as admirable.

I do not pretend to taste, but I am sincere; nor do I endeavour to be consistent. Consistency does not interest me.

The only consistency possible is a consistency which comes from without, which proceeds from fear of public opinion, and anything of this sort appears to me to be contemptible.

Not to change because of what others may think, is one of the most abject forms of slavery.

Let us change all we can. My ideal is continual change—change of life, change of home, of food, and even of skin.

MY LIBRARY

Among the things that I missed most as a student, was a small library. If I had had one, I believe I should have dipped more deeply into books and into life as well; but it was not given me. During the period which is most fruitful for the maturing of the mind, that is, during the years from twelve to twenty, I lived by turns in six or seven cities, and as it was impossible to travel about with books, I never retained any.

A lack of books was the occasion of my failure to form the habit of re-reading, of tasting again and again and of relishing what I read, and also of making notes in the margin.

Nearly all authors who own a small library, in which the books are properly arranged, and nicely annotated, become famous.

I am not sentimentalizing about stolid, brazen note-taking, such as that with which the gentlemen of the Ateneo debase their books, because that merely indicates barbarous lack of culture and an obtuseness which is Kabyline.

Having had no library in my youth, I have never possessed the old favourites that everybody carries in his pocket into the country, and reads over and over until he knows them by heart.

I have looked in and out of books as travellers do in and out of inns, not stopping long in any of them. I am very sorry but it is too late now for the loss to be repaired.

ON BEING A GENTLEMAN

Viewed from without, I seem to impress some as a crass, crabbed person, who has very little ability, while others regard me as an unhealthy, decadent writer. Then Azorín has said of me that I am a literary aristocrat, a fine and comprehensive mind.

I should accept Azorín's opinion very gladly, but personality needs to be hammered severely in literature before it leaves its slag. Like metal which is removed from the furnace after casting and placed under the hammer, I would offer my works to be put to the test, to be beaten by all hammers.

If anything were left, I should treasure it then lovingly; if nothing were left, we should still pick up some fragments of life.

I always listen to the opinions of the non-literary concerning my books with the greatest interest. My cousin, Justo Goñi, used to express his opinion without circumlocution. He always carried off my books as they appeared, and then, a long time after, would give his opinion.

Of *The Way of Perfection* he said:

"Good, yes, very good; but it is so tiresome."

I realized that there was some truth in his view.

When he read the three novels to which I had given the general title, *The Struggle for Life*, he stopped me on the Calle de Alcalá one day and said:

"You have not convinced me."

"How so?"

"Your hero is a man of the people, but he is falsified. He is just like you are; you can never be anything but a gentleman."

This gentility with which my cousin reproached me, and without doubt he was correct, is common to nearly all Spanish writers.

There are no Spaniards at present, and there never have been any at any other time, who write out of the Spanish soul, out of the hearts of the people. Even Dicenta did not. His *Juan José* is not a workingman, but a young gentleman. He has nothing of the workingman about him beyond the label, the clothes, and such externals.

Galdós, for example, can make the common people talk; Azorín can portray the villages of Castile, set on their arid heights, against backgrounds of blue skies; Blasco Ibáñez can paint the life of the Valencians in vivid colours with a prodigality that carries with it the taint of the cheap, but none of them has penetrated into the popular soul. That would require a great poet, and we have none.

GIVING OFFENCE

I have the name of being aggressive, but, as a matter of fact, I have scarcely ever attacked any one personally.

Many hold a radical opinion to be an insult.

In an article in *La Lectura*, Ortega y Gasset illustrates my propensity to become offensive by recalling that as we left the Ateneo together one afternoon, we encountered a blind man on the Calle del Prado, singing a *jota*, whereupon I remarked: "An unspeakable song!"

Admitted. It is a fact, but I fail to see any cause of offence. It is only another way of saying more forcefully: "I do not like it, it does not please me," or what you will.

I have often been surprised to find, after expressing an opinion, that I have been insulted bitterly in reply.

At the outset of my literary career, Azorín and I shared the ill will of everybody.

When Maeztu, Azorín, Carlos del Rio and myself edited a modest magazine, by the name of *Juventud*, Azorín and I were the ones principally to be insulted. The experience was repeated later when we were both associated with *El Globo*.

Azorín, perhaps, was attacked and insulted more frequently, so that I was often in a position to act as his champion.

Some years ago I published an article in the *Nuevo Mundo*, in which I considered Vázquez Mella and his refutation of the Kantian philosophy, dwelling especially upon his seventeenth mathematical proof of the existence of God. The thing was a burlesque, but a conservative paper took issue with me, called me an atheist, a plagiarist, a drunkard and an ass. As for being an atheist, I did not take that as an insult, but as an honour.

Upon another occasion, I published an article about Spanish women, with particular reference to Basque women, in which I maintained that they sacrificed natural kindliness and sympathy on the altars of honour and religion, whereupon the Daughters of Mary of San Sebastian made answer, charging that I was a degenerate son of their city, who had robbed them of their honour, which was absolutely contrary to the fact. In passing, they suggested to the editor of the *Nuevo Mundo* that he should not permit me to write again for the magazine.

I wrote an article once dealing with Maceo and Cuba, whereupon a journalist from those parts jumped up and called me a fat Basque ox.

The Catalans have also obliged me with some choice insults, which I have found engaging. When I lectured in Barcelona in the Casa del Pueblo, *La Veu de Catalunya* undertook to report the affair, picturing me as talking platitudes before an audience of professional bomb throwers and dynamiters, and experts with the Browning gun.

Naturally, I was enchanted.

Recently, when writing for the review *España*, I had a similar experience, which reminded me of my connection with the smaller periodicals of fifteen years ago. Some gentlemen, mostly natives of the provinces, approached the editor, Ortega y Gasset, with the information that I was not a fit person to contribute to a serious magazine, as what I wrote was not so, while my name would ruin the sale of the weekly.

These pious souls and good Christians imagined that I might need that work in order to earn my living, so in the odour of sanctity they did whatever lay in their power to deprive me of my means of support. Oh, noble souls! Oh, ye of great heart! I salute you from a safe distance, and wish you the most uncomfortable beds in the most intolerable wards set apart for scurvy patients, in any hospital of your choosing, throughout the world.

THIRST FOR GLORY

Fame, success, popularity, the illusion of being known, admired and esteemed, appeal in different ways to authors. To Salvador Rueda, glory is a triumphant entrance into Tegucigalpa, where he is taken to the Spanish Casino, and crowned with a crown of real laurel. To Unamuno, glory is the assurance that people will be interested in him at least a thousand years after he is dead. And to others the only glory worth talking about is that courted by the French writer, Rabbe, who busied himself in Spain with la *gloire argent comptant*. Some yearn for a large stage with pennons and salvos and banners, while others are content with a smaller scene.

Ortega y Gasset says that to me glory reduces itself to the proportions of an agreeable dinner, with good talk across the table.

And he is right. To mingle with pleasant, intelligent, cordial persons is one of the more alluring sorts of fame.

There is something seductive and ingratiating about table talk when it is spirited. A luxurious dining room, seating eight or ten guests, of whom three or four are pretty women, one of whom should be a foreigner; as many men, none of them aristocrats—generally speaking, aristocrats are disagreeable— nor shall we admit artists, for they are in the same class as the aristocrats; one's neighbour, perhaps, is a banker, or a Jew of aquiline feature, and then the talk touches on life and on politics, relieved with a little gallantry toward the ladies, from time to time allowing to each his brief opportunity to shine— all this, beyond doubt, is most agreeable.

I like, too, to spend an afternoon conversing with a number of ladies in a comfortable drawing room, which is well heated. I visualize the various rewards which are meted out by fame as being housed invariably under a good roof. What is not intimate, does not appeal to me.

I have often seen Guimerá in a café on the Rambla in Barcelona, drinking coffee at a table, alone and forlorn, in the midst of a crowd of shop clerks and commercial travellers.

"Is that Guimerá?" I asked a Catalan journalist.

"Yes."

And then he told me that they had tendered him a tremendous testimonial some months previously, which had been attended by I don't know how many hundreds of societies, all marching with their banners.

I have no very clear idea of just what Guimerá has done, as it is many years since I have gone to the theatre, but I know that he is considered in Catalonia to be one of the glories of the country.

I should not care for an apotheosis, and then find myself left forlorn and alone to take my coffee afterwards with a horde of clerks.

I may never write anything that will take the world by storm—most probably not; but if I do, and it occurs to my fellow townsmen to organize one of these celebrations with flags, banners and choral societies, they need not count upon my attendance. They will not be able to discover me even with the aid of Sherlock Holmes.

When I am old, I hope to take coffee with pleasant friends, whether it be in a palace or a porter's lodge. I neither expect nor desire flags, committees, nor waving banners.

Laurel does not seduce me, and you cannot do it with bunting.

ELECTIVE ANTIPATHIES

As I have expressed my opinions of other authors sharply, making them public with the proper disgust, others have done the same with me, which is but logical and natural, especially in the case of a writer such as myself, who holds that sympathy and antipathy are of the very essence of art.

My opponents and myself differ chiefly in the fact that I am more cynical than they, and so I disclose my personal animus quite ingenuously, which my enemies fail to do.

I hold that there are two kinds of morality; morality of work and morality of play. The morality of work is an immoral morality, which teaches us to take advantage of circumstances and to lie. The morality of play, for the reason that it deals with mere futilities, is finer and more chivalrous.

I believe that in literature and in all liberal arts, the morality should be the morality of play, while my opponents for the most part hold that the morality of literature should be the morality of work. I have never, consciously at least, been influenced in my literary opinions by practical considerations. My ideas may have been capricious, and they are,—they may even be bad,—but they have no ulterior practical motive.

My failure to be practical, together, perhaps, with an undue obtuseness of perception, brings me face to face with critics of two sorts: one, esthetic; the other, social.

My esthetic critics say to me:

"You have not perfected your style, you have not developed the technique of your novels. You can scarcely be said to be literate."

I shrug my shoulders and reply: "Are you sure?"

My social critics reproach me for my negative and destructive views. I do not know how to create anything, I am incapable of enthusiasm, I cannot describe life, and so on.

This feeling seems logical enough, if it is sincere, if it is honest, and I accept it as such, and it does not offend me.

But, as some of my esthetic critics tell me: "You are not an artist, you do not know how to write," without feeling any deep conviction on the subject, but rather fearing that perhaps I may be an artist after all and that at last somebody may come to think so, so among my critics who pose as defenders of society, there are those who are influenced by motives which are purely utilitarian.

I am reminded of servants shouting at a man picking flowers over the garden wall, or an apple from the orchard as he passes, who raise their voices as high as possible so as to make their officiousness known.

They shout so that their masters will hear.

"How dare that rascal pick flowers from the garden? How dare he defy us and our masters? Shall a beggar, who is not respectable, tell us that our laws are not laws, that our honours are not honours, and that we are a gang of accomplished idiots?"

Yes, that is just what I tell them, and I shall continue to do so as long as it is the truth.

Shout, you lusty louts in gaudy liveries, bark you little lap-dogs, guard the gates, you government inspectors and carabineers! I shall look into your garden, which is also my garden, I shall make off with anything from it that I am able, and I shall say what I please.

TO A MEMBER OF SEVERAL ACADEMIES

A certain Basque writer, one Señor de Loyarte, who is a member of several academies, and Royal Commissioner of Education, assails me violently upon social grounds in a book which he has published, although the attack is veiled as purely literary.

Señor de Loyarte is soporific as a general rule, but in his polite sortie against me, he is more amusing than is usual. His malice is so keen that it very nearly causes him to appear intelligent.

In literature, Señor de Loyarte—and why should Señor de Loyarte not be associated with literature—presents the figure of a fat, pale, flabby boy in a priests' school, skulking under the skirts of a Jesuit Father.

Señor de Loyarte, like those little, chubby-winged cherubs on sacristy ceilings, shakes his arrowlet at me and lets fling a *billet doux*.

Señor de Loyarte says I smack of the cadaver, that I am a plagiarist, an atheist, anti-religious, anti-patriotic, and more to boot.

I shall not reply for it may be true. Yet it is also true that Señor de Loyarte's noble words will please his noble patrons, from whom, perhaps, he may receive applause even more substantial than the pat on the shoulder of a Jesuit Father, or the smile of every good Conservative, who is a defender of the social order. His book is an achievement which should induct Señor de Loyarte into membership in several more academies. Señor de Loyarte is already a Corresponding Member of the Spanish Academy, or of the Academy of History, I am not quite sure which; but they are all the same. Speaking of history, I should be interested to know who did first introduce the sponge.

Señor de Loyarte is destined to be a member, a member of academies all his life.

IV

ADMIRATIONS AND INCOMPATIBILITIES

Diogenes Laertius tells us that when Zeno consulted the oracle as to what he should do in order to attain happiness in life, the deity replied that he should assimilate himself with the dead. Having understood, he applied himself exclusively to the study of books.

Thus speaks Laertius, in the translation of Don José Ortíz y Sanz. I confess that I should not have understood the oracle. However, without consulting any oracle, I have devoted myself for some time to reading books, whether ancient and modern, both out of curiosity and in order to learn something of life.

CERVANTES, SHAKESPEARE, MOLIÈRE

For a long time, I thought that Shakespeare was a writer who was unique and different from all others. It seemed to me that the difference between him and other writers was one of quality rather than of quantity. I felt that, as a man, Shakespeare was of a different kind of humanity; but I do not think so now. Shakespeare is no more the quintessence of the world's literature than Plato and Kant are the quintessence of universal philosophy. I once admired the philosophy and characters of the author of Hamlet; when I read him today, what most impresses me is his rhetoric, and, above all, his high spirit.

Cervantes is not very sympathetic to me. He is tainted with the perfidy of the man who has made a pact with the enemy (with the Church, the aristocracy, with those in power), and then conceals the fact. Philosophically, in spite of his enthusiasm for the Renaissance, he appears vulgar and pedestrian to me, although he towers above all his contemporaries on account of the success of a single invention, that of Don Quixote and Sancho, which is to literature what the discovery of Newton was to Physics.

As for Molière, he is a poor fellow, who never attains the exuberance of Shakespeare, nor the invention that immortalizes Cervantes. But his taste is better than Shakespeare's and he is more social, more modern than Cervantes. The half-century or more that separates the work of Cervantes from that of Molière, is not sufficient to explain this modernity. Between the Spain of *Quixote* and the France of *Le Bourgeois Gentilhomme*, lies something deeper than time. Descartes and Gassendi had lived in France, while, on the other hand, the seed of Saint Ignatius Loyola lay germinating in the Spain of Cervantes.

THE ENCYCLOPEDISTS

A French journalist who visited my house during the summer, remarked:

"The ideas were great in the French Revolution; it was not the men." I replied: "I believe that the men of the French Revolution were great, but not the ideas."

Of all the philosophical literature of the pre-revolutionary period, what remains today?

What books exert influence? In France, excerpts from Montesquieu, Diderot and Rousseau are still read in the schools, but outside of France, they are read nowhere.

Only an extraordinary person would go away for the summer with Montesquieu's *Esprit des Lois*, or Jean Jacques Rousseau's *Emile* in his grip. Montesquieu is demonstration of the fact that a book cannot live entirely by virtue of correctness of style.

Of all the writers who enjoyed such fame in the eighteenth century, the only one who will bear reading today is Voltaire—the Voltaire of the *Dictionnaire Philosophique* and of the novels.

Diderot, whom the French consider a great man, is of no interest whatsoever to the modern mind, at least to the mind which is not French. He is almost as dull as Rousseau. *La Religieuse* is an utterly false little book. Some years ago I loaned a copy to a young lady who had just come from a convent. "I have never seen anything like this," she said to me. "It is a fantasy with no relation to the truth." That was my idea. *Jacques, le fataliste* is tiresome; *Le Neveu de Rameau* gives at first the impression that it is going to amount to something, to something powerful such as the *Satiricon* of Petronius, or *El Buscón* of Quevedo; but at the end, it is nothing.

The only writer of the pre-revolutionary period who can be read today with any pleasure—and this, perhaps, is because he does not attempt anything—is Chamfort. His characters and anecdotes are sufficiently highly flavoured to defy the action of time.

THE ROMANTICISTS

Goethe

If a militia of genius should be formed on Parnassus, Goethe would be the drum-major. He is so great, so majestic, so serene, so full of talent, so abounding in virtue, and yet, so antipathetic!

Chateaubriand

A skin of Lacrymae Christi that has turned sour. At times the good Viscount drops molasses into the skin to take away the taste of vinegar; at other times, he drops in more vinegar to take away the sweet taste of the molasses. He is both moth-eaten and sublime.

Victor Hugo

Victor Hugo, the most talented of rhetoricians! Victor Hugo, the most exquisite of vulgarians! Victor Hugo—mere common sense dressed up as art.

Stendhal

The inventor of a psychological automaton moved by clock work.

Balzac

A nightmare, a dream produced by indigestion, a chill, rare acuteness, equal obtuseness, a delirium of splendours, cheap hardware, of pretence and bad taste. Because of his ugliness, because of his genius, because of his immorality, the Danton of printers' ink.

Poe

A mysterious sphinx who makes one tremble with lynx-like eyes, the goldsmith of magical wonders.

Dickens

At once a mystic and a sad clown. The Saint Vincent de Paul of the loosened string, the Saint Francis of Assisi of the London Streets. Everything is gesticulation, and the gesticulations are ambiguous. When we think he is going to weep, he laughs; when we think he is going to laugh, he cries. A remarkable genius who does everything he can to make himself appear puny, yet who is, beyond doubt, very great.

Larra [Footnote: A Spanish poet and satirist (1809-37), famous under the pseudonym of Figaro. He committed suicide. The poet Zorrilla first came into prominence through some verses read at his tomb.]

A small, trained tiger shut up in a tiny cage. He has all the tricks of a cat; he mews like one, he lets you stroke his back, and there are times when his fiercer instincts show in his eyes. Then you realize that he is thinking: "How I should love to eat you up!"

THE NATURALISTS

Flaubert

Flaubert is a heavy-footed animal. It is plain that he is a Norman. All his work has great specific gravity. He disgusts me. One of Flaubert's master strokes was the conception of the character of Homais, the apothecary, in *Madame Bovary*. I cannot see, however, that Homais is any more stupid than Flaubert himself, and he may even be less so.

The Giants

The good Zola, vigorous, dull and perspiring, dubbed his contemporaries, the French naturalistic novelists, "Giants." What an imagination was possessed by Zola!

These "Giants" were none other than the Goncourts, whose insignificance approached at times imbecility, and in addition, Alphonse Daudet, with the air of a cheap comedian and an armful of mediocre books—a truly French diet, feeble, but well seasoned. These poor Giants, of whom Zola would talk, have become so weak and shrunken with time, that nobody is able any longer to make them out, even as dwarfs.

THE SPANISH REALISTS

The Spanish realists of the same period are the height of the disagreeable. The most repugnant of them all is Pereda. When I read him, I feel as if I were riding on a balky, vicious mule, which proceeds at an uncomfortable little trot, and then, all of a sudden, cuts stilted capers like a circus horse.

THE RUSSIANS

Dostoievski

One hundred years hence Dostoievsky's appearance in literature will be hailed as one of the most extraordinary events of the nineteenth century. Among the spiritual fauna of Europe, his place will be that of the Diplodocus.

Tolstoi

A number of years ago I was in the habit of visiting the Ateneo, and I used to argue there with the habitués, who in general have succeeded in damming up the channels through which other men receive ideas.

"To my mind, Tolstoi is a Greek," I observed. "He is serene, clear, his characters are god-like; all they think of are their love affairs, their passions. They are never called upon to face the acute problem of subsistence, which is fundamental with us."

"Utter nonsense! There is nothing Greek about Tolstoi," declared everybody.

Some years later at a celebration in honour of Tolstoi, Anatole France chanced to remark: "Tolstoi is a Greek."

When this fell from Anatole France, the obstruction in the channels through which these gentlemen of the Ateneo received their ideas ceased for the moment to exist, and they began to believe that, after all, Tolstoi might very well have something of the Greek in him.

THE CRITICS

Sainte Beuve

Sainte Beuve writes as if he had always said the last word, as if he were precisely at the needle of the scales. Yet I feel that this writer is not as infallible as he thinks. His interest lies in his anecdote, in his malevolent insinuation, in his bawdry. Beyond these, he has the same Mediterranean features as the rest of us.

Taine

Hippolyte Taine is also one of those persons who think they understand everything. And there are times when he understands nothing. His *History of English Literature*, which makes an effort to be broad and generous, is one of the pettiest, most niggardly histories ever written anywhere. His articles on Shakespeare, Walter Scott and Dickens have been fabricated by a French professor, which is to say that they are among the most wooden productions of the universities of Europe.

Ruskin

He impresses me as the Prince of Upstarts, grandiloquent and at the same time unctuous, a General in a Salvation Army of Art, or a monk who is a devotee of an esthetic Doctrine which has been drawn up by a Congress of Tourists.

Croce

The esthetic theory of Benedetto Croce has proved another delusion to me. Rather than an esthetic theory, it is a study of esthetic theories. As in most Latin productions, the fundamental question is not discussed therein, but the method of approaching that question.

Clarin [Footnote: Pseudonym of Leopoldo Alas, a Spanish critic and novelist of the transition, born in Asturias, whose influence was widely felt in Spanish letters. He died in 1905.]

I have a poor opinion of Clarin, although some of my friends regard him with admiration. As a man, he must have been envious; as a novelist, he is dull and unhappy; as a critic, I am not certain that he was ever in the right.

V

THE PHILOSOPHERS

A thirst for some knowledge of philosophy resulted in consulting Dr. Letamendi's book on pathology during my student days. I also purchased the works of Kant, Fichte, and Schopenhauer in the cheap editions which were published by Zozaya. The first of these that I read was Fichte's *Science of Knowledge*, of which I understood nothing. It stirred in me a veritable indignation against both author and translator. Was philosophy nothing but mystification, as it is assumed to be by artists and shop clerks?

Reading *Parerga and Paralipomena* reconciled me to philosophy. After that I bought in French *The Critique of Pure Reason*, *The World as Will and Idea*, and a number of other books.

How was it that I, who am gifted with but little tenacity of purpose, mustered up perseverance enough to read difficult books for which I was without preparation? I do not know, but the fact is that I read them.

Years after this initiation into philosophy, I began reading the works of Nietzsche, which impressed me greatly.

Since then I have picked at this and that in order to renew my philosophic store, but without success. Some books and authors will not agree with me, and I have not dared to venture others. I have had a volume of Hegel's *Logic* on my table for a long time. I have looked at it, I have smelled of it, but courage fails me.

Yet I am attracted to metaphysics more than to any other phase of philosophy. Political philosophy, sociology and the common sense schools please me least. Hobbes, Locke, Bentham, Comte and Spencer I have never liked at all. Even their Utopias, which ought to be amusing, bore me profoundly, and this has been true from Plato's *Republic* to Kropotkin's *Conquest of Bread* and Wells's *A Modern Utopia*. Nor could I ever become interested in the pseudo-philosophy of anarchism. One of the books which have disappointed me the most is Max Stirner's *Ego and His Own*.

Psychology is a science which I should like to know. I have therefore skimmed through the standard works of Wundt and Ziehen. After reading them, I came to the conclusion that the psychology which I am seeking, day by day and every day, is not to be found in these treatises. It is contained rather in the writings of Nietzsche and the novels of Dostoievski. In the course of time, I may succeed, perhaps, in entering the more abstract domains of the science.

VI

THE HISTORIANS

Miss Blimber, the school teacher in Dickens's *Dombey and Son*, could have died happily had she known Cicero. Even if such a thing were possible I should have no great desire to know Cicero, but I should be glad to listen to a lecture by Zeno in the portico of the Poecilé at Athens, or to Epicurus's meditations in his garden.

My ignorance of history has prevented me from becoming deeply interested in Greece, although now this begins to embarrass me, as a curiosity about and sympathy for classical art stirs within me. If I were a young man and had the leisure, I might even begin the study of Greek.

As it is, I feel that there are two Greeces: one of statues and temples, which is academic and somewhat cold; the other of philosophers and tragedians, who convey to my mind more of an impression of life and humanity.

Apart from the Greek, which I know but fragmentarily, I have no great admiration for ancient literatures. The *Old Testament* never aroused any devotion in me. Except for *Ecclesiastes* and one or two of the shorter books, it impresses me as repulsively cruel and antipathetic.

Among the Greeks, I have enjoyed Homer's *Odyssey* and the comedies of Aristophanes. I have read also Herodotus, Plutarch and Diogenes Laertius. I am not an admirer of academic, well written books, so I prefer Diogenes Laertius to Plutarch. Plutarch impresses me as having composed and arranged his narratives; not so Diogenes Laertius. Plutarch forces the morality of his personages to the fore; Diogenes gives details of both the good and the bad in his. Plutarch is solid and systematic; Diogenes is lighter and lacks system. I prefer Diogenes Laertius to Plutarch, and if I were especially interested in any of the illustrious ancients of whom they write, I should vastly prefer the letters of the men themselves, if any existed, or otherwise the gossip of their tentmakers or washerwomen, to any lives written of them by either Diogenes Laertius or Plutarch.

THE ROMAN HISTORIANS

When I turned to the composition of historical novels, I desired to ascertain if the historical method had been reduced to a system. I read Lucian's *Instructions for Writing History*, an essay with the same title, or with a very similar one, by the Abbé Mably, some essays by Simmel, besides a book by a German professor, Ernst Bernheim, *Lehrbuch der historischen Methode*.

I next read and re-read the Roman historians Julius Caesar, Tacitus, Sallust and Suetonius.

Sallust

All these Roman historians no doubt were worthy gentlemen, but they create an atmosphere of suspicion. When reading them, you suspect that they are not always telling the whole truth. I read Sallust and feel that he is lying; he has composed his narrative like a novel.

In the *Mémorial de Sainte Hélène*, it is recorded that on March 26, 1816, Napoleon read the conspiracy of Catiline in the *Roman History*. The Emperor observed that he was unable to understand what Catiline was driving at. No matter how much of a bandit he may have been, he must have had some object, some social purpose in view.

The observation of this political genius is one which must occur to all who read Sallust's book. How could Catiline have secured the support of the most brilliant men of Rome, among them of Julius Caesar, if his only plan and object had been to loot and burn Rome? It is not logical. Evidently Sallust lies, as governmental writers in Spain lie today when they speak of Lerroux or Ferrer, or as the republican supporters of Thiers lied in 1871, characterizing the Paris Commune.

Tacitus

Tacitus is another great Roman historian who is theatrical, melodramatic, solemn, full of grand gestures. He also creates an atmosphere of suspicion, of falsehood. Tacitus has something of the inquisitor in him, of the fanatic in the cause of virtue. He is a man of austere moral attitude, which is a pose that a thoroughgoing scamp finds it easy to assume.

A temperament such as that of Tacitus is fatal to theatrical peoples like the Italians, Spaniards, and French of the South. From it springs that type of Sicilian, Calabrian, and Andalusian politician who is a great lawyer and an eloquent orator, who declaims publicly in the forum, and then reaches an understanding privately with bandits and thugs.

Suetonius

Suetonius, although deficient both in the pomp and sententiousness of Tacitus, makes no attempt to compose his story, nor to impart moral instruction, but tells us what he knows, simply. His *Lives of the Twelve Caesars* is the greatest collection of horrors in history. You leave it with the imagination perturbed, scrutinizing yourself to discover whether you may not be yourself a hog or a wild beast. Suetonius gives us an account of men rather than a history of the politics of emperors, and surely this method is more interesting and veracious. I place more faith in the anecdotes which grow up about an historical figure than I do in his laws.

Polybius is a mixture of scepticism and common sense. He is what Bayle, Montesquieu and Voltaire will come to be centuries hence.

As far as Caesar's *Commentaries* are concerned, in spite of the fact that they have been manipulated very skilfully, they are one of the most satisfying and instructive books that can be read.

MODERN AND CONTEMPORARY HISTORIANS

I have very little knowledge of the historians of the Renaissance or of those prior to the French Revolution. Apart from the chroniclers of individual exploits, such as López de Ayala, Brantôme, and the others, they are wholly colourless, and either pseudo-Roman or pseudo-Greek. Even Machiavelli has a personal, Italian side, which is mocking and incisive—and this is all that is worth while in him—and he has a pretentious pseudo-Roman side, which is unspeakably tiresome.

Generally considered, the more carefully composed and smoothly varnished the history, the duller it will be found; while the more personal revelations it contains, the more engaging. Most readers today, for example, prefer Bernal Díaz del Castillo's *True History of the Conquest of New Spain* to Solis's *History of the Conquest of Mexico*. One is the book of a soldier, who had a share in the deeds described, and who reveals himself for what he is, with all his prejudices, vanities and arrogance; the other is a scholar's attempt to imitate a classic history and to maintain a monotonous music throughout his paragraphs.

Practically all the historians who have followed the French Revolution have individual character, and some have too much of it, as has Carlyle. They distort their subject until it becomes a pure matter of fantasy, or mere literature, or sinks even to the level of a family discussion.

Macaulay's moral pedantry, Thiers's cold and repulsive cretinism, the melodramatic, gesticulatory effusiveness of Michelet are all typical styles.

Historical bazaars *à la* Cesare Cantù may be put on one side, as belonging to an inferior genre. They remind me of those great nineteenth century world's fairs, vast, miscellaneous and exhausting.

As for the German historians, they are not translated, so I do not know them. I have read only a few essays of Simmel, which I think extremely keen, and Stewart Chamberlain's book upon the foundations of the nineteenth century, which, if the word France were to be substituted for the word Germany, might easily have been the production of an advanced nationalist of the *Action Française*.

VII

MY FAMILY

FAMILY MYTHOLOGY

The celebrated Vicomte de Chateaubriand, after flaunting an ancestry of princes and kings in his *Memoires d'outre-tombe*, then turns about and tells us that he attaches no importance to such matters.

I shall do the same. I intend to furbish up our family history and mythology, and then I shall assert that I attach no importance to them. And, what is more, I shall be telling the truth.

My researches into the life of Aviraneta [Footnote: A kinsman of Baroja and protagonist of his series of historical novels under the general title of *Memoirs of a Man of Action*.] have drawn me of late to the genealogical field, and I have looked into my family, which is equivalent to compounding with tradition and even with reaction.

I have unearthed three family myths: the Goñi myth, the Zornoza myth, and the Alzate myth.

The Goñi myth, vouched for by an aunt of mine who died in San Sebastian at an age of ninety or more, established, according to her, that she was a descendant of Don Teodosio de Goñi, a Navarrese *caballero* who lived in the time of Witiza, and who, after killing his father and mother at the instigation of the devil, betook himself to Mount Aralar wearing an iron ring about his neck, and dragging a chain behind him, thus pilloried to do penance. One day, a terrible dragon appeared before him during a storm.

Don Teodosio lifted up his soul unto God, and thereupon the Archangel Saint Michael revealed himself to him, in his dire extremity, and broke his chains, in commemoration of which event Don Teodosio caused to be erected the chapel of San Miguel in Excelsis on Mount Aralar.

There were those who endeavoured to convince my aunt that in the time of this supposititious Don Teodosio, which was the early part of the eighth century, surnames had not come into use in the Basque country, and even, indeed, that there were at that time no Christians there—in short they maintained that Don Teodosio was a solar myth; but they were not able to convince my aunt. She had seen the chapel of San Miguel on Aralar, and the cave in which the dragon lived, and a document wherein Charles V. granted to Juan de Goñi the privilege of renaming his house the Palace of San Miguel, as well as of adding a dragon to his coat of arms, besides a cross in a red field, and a *broken* chain.

The Zornoza myth was handed down through my paternal grandmother of that name.

I remember having heard this lady say when I was a child, that her family might be traced in a direct line to the chancellor Pero López de Ayala, and, I know not through what lateral branches, also to St. Francis Xavier.

My grandmother vouched for the fact that her father had sold the documents and parchments in which these details were set forth, to a titled personage from Madrid.

The Zornozas boast an escutcheon which is embellished with a band, a number of wolves, and a legend whose import I do not recall.

Indeed, wolves occur in all the escutcheons of the Baroja, Alzate and Zornoza families, in so far as I have been able to discover, and I take them to be more or less authentic. We have wolves passant, wolves rampant, and wolves mordant. The Goñi escutcheon also displays hearts. If I become rich, which I do not anticipate, I shall have wolves and hearts blazoned on the doors of my dazzling automobile, which will not prevent me from enjoying myself hugely inside of it.

Turning to the Alzate myth, it too runs back to antiquity and the primitive struggles of rival families of Navarre and Labourt. The Alzates have been lords of Vera ever since the fourteenth century.

The legend of the Alzates of Vera de Navarra relates that one Don Rodrigo, master of the village in the fifteenth century, fell in love with a daughter of the house of Urtubi, in France, near Urruña, and married her. Don Rodrigo went to live in Urtubi and became so thoroughly gallicized that he never cared to return to Spain, so the people of Vera banded together, dispossessed him of his honours and dignity, and sequestrated his lands.

In the early part of the nineteenth century, my great-grandfather, Sebastián Ignacio de Alzate, was among those who assembled at Zubieta in 1813 to take part in the rebuilding of San Sebastian, and this great-grandfather was uncle to Don Eugenio de Aviraneta, a good relative of mine, protagonist of my latest books.

St. Francis Xavier, Don Teodosio de Goñi, Pero López de Ayala, Aviraneta—a saint, a revered worthy, an historian, a conspirator—these are our family gods.

Now let me take my stand with Chateaubriand as attaching no importance to such things.

OUR HISTORY

Baroja is a hamlet in the province of Alava in the district of Peñacerrada. According to Fernández Guerra, it is an Iberian name derived from Asiatic Iberia. I believe that I have read in Campión that the word Baroja is compounded from the Celtic *bar*, meaning mountain, and the Basque *otza*, *ocha* meaning cold. In short, a cold mountain.

The district of Peñacerrada, which includes Baroja, is an austere land, covered with intricate mountain ranges which are clad with trees and scrub live oaks.

Hawks abound. In his treatise on falconry, Zúñiga mentions the Bahari falcon, propagated principally among the mountains of Peñacerrada.

My ancestors originally called themselves Martínez de Baroja. One Martín had a son who was known as Martínez. This Martínez (son of Martín) doubtless left the village, and as there were others of the name Martínez (sons of Martín), they dubbed him the Martínez of Baroja, or Martínez de Baroja.

The Martínez de Barojas lived in that country for many years; they were hidalgos, Christians of old stock. And there is still a family of the name in Peñacerrada.

One Martínez de Baroja, by name Juan, who lived in the village of Samiano, upon becoming outraged because of an attempt to force him to pay tribute to the Count of Salinas—in those days a very natural source of offence—took an appeal in the year 1616 from a ruling of the Prosecuting Attorney of His Majesty and the Alcaldes and Regidors of the Earldom of Treviño, and he was sustained by the Chamber of Hidalgos at Valladolid, which decided in his favour in a decree dated the eighth day of the month of August, 1619.

This same hidalgo, Juan Martínez de Baroja, moved the enforcement of this decree, as is affirmed by a writ of execution which is inscribed on forty-five leaves of parchment, to which is attached a leaden seal pendant from a cord of silk, at the end of which may be found the stipulations of the judgment entered against the Municipality and Corporation of the Town and Earldom of Treviño and the Village of Samiano.

The Martínez de Barojas, despite the fact that they sprang from the land of the falcon and the hawk, in temper must have been dark, heavy, rough. They were members of the Brotherhood of San Martín de Peñacerrada, which apparently was of great account in those regions, besides being regidors and alcaldes of the Santa Hermandad, a rural police and judicial organization which extended throughout the country.

In the eighteenth century, one of the family, my great-grandfather Rafael, doubtless possessing more initiative, or having more of the hawk in him than the others, grew tired of ploughing up the earth, and left the village, turning pharmacist, setting up in 1803 at Oyarzun, in Guipúzcoa. This Rafael shortened his name and signed himself Rafael de Baroja.

Don Rafael must have been a man of modern sympathies, for he bought a printing press and began to issue pamphlets and even occasional books.

Evidently Don Rafael was also a man of radical ideas. He published a newspaper at San Sebastian in 1822 and 1823, which he called *El Liberal Guipúzcoano*. I have seen only one copy of this, and that was in the National Library.

That this newspaper was extremely liberal, may be judged by the articles that were reprinted from it in *El Espectador*, the Masonic journal published at Madrid during the period. Don Rafael had connections both with constitutionalists and members of the Gallic party. There must have been antecedents of a liberal character in our family, as Don Rafael's uncle, Don Juan José de Baroja, at first a priest at Pipaon and later at Vitoria, had been enrolled in the Basque *Sociedad Económica*.

Don Rafael had two sons, Ignacio Ramón and Pío. They settled in San Sebastian as printers. Pío was my grandfather.

My second family name, Nessi, as I have said before, comes out of Lombardy and the city of Como.

The Nessis of Como fled from Austrian rule, and came to Spain, probably peddling mousetraps and *santi boniti barati*.

One of the Nessis, who survived until a short time ago, always said that the family had been very comfortably off in Lombardy, where one of his relatives, Guiseppe Nessi, a doctor, had been professor in the University of Pavia during the eighteenth century, besides being major in the Austrian Army.

As mementos of the Italian branch of the family, I still preserve a few views of Lake Como in my house, a crude image of the Christ of the Annunziatta, stamped on cloth, and a volume of a treatise on surgery by Nessi, which bears the *imprimatur* of the Inquisition at Venice.

VIII

MEMORIES OF CHILDHOOD

SAN SEBASTIAN

I was born in San Sebastian on the 28th of December, 1872. So I am not only a Guipúzcoan but a native of San Sebastian. The former I regard as an honour, but the latter means very little to me.

I should prefer to have been born in a mountain hamlet or in a small coast town, rather than in a city of summer visitors and hotel keepers.

Garat, who was a most conventional person who lived in Bayonne, always used to maintain that he came from Ustariz. I might say that I am from Vera del Bidasoa, but I should not deceive myself.

There are several reasons why I dislike San Sebastian:

In the first place, the city is not beautiful, when it might well be so. It is made up of straight streets which are all alike, together with two or three monuments that are horrible. The general construction is miserable and shoddy. Although excellent stone abounds in the neighbourhood, no one has had the sense to erect anything either noble or dignified. Cheap houses confront the eye on all sides, whether simple or pretentious. Whenever the citizens of San Sebastian raise their hands—and in this they are abetted by the *Madrileños*—they do something ugly. They have defaced Monte Igueldo already, and now they are defacing the Castillo. Tomorrow, they will manage somehow to spoil the sea, the sky, and the air.

As for the spirit of the city, it is lamentable. There is no interest in science, art, literature, history, politics, or anything else. All that the inhabitants think about are the King, the Queen Regent, yachts, bull fights, and the latest fashions in trousers.

San Sebastian is a conglomeration of parvenus and upstarts from Pamplona, Saragossa, Valladolid, Chile and Chuquisaca, who are anxious to show themselves off. Some do this by walking alongside of the King, or by taking coffee with a famous bull-fighter, or by bowing to some aristocrat. The young men of San Sebastian are among the most worthless in Spain. I have always looked upon them as *infra* human.

As for the ladies, many of them might be taken for princesses in summer, but their winter tertulias are on a level with a porter's lodge where they play *julepe*. It is a card game, but the word means dose, and Madame Recamier would have fainted at the mention of it.

When I observe these parvenus' attempts to shine, I think to myself: "The ostentation of the freshman year at college. How unfortunate that some of us have moved on to the doctorate!"

No one reads in San Sebastian. They run over the society news, and then drop the paper for fear their brains will begin to smoke.

This city, imagining itself to be so cultivated, although it really is a new town, is under the domination of a few Jesuit fathers, who, like most of the present days sons of Loyola, are coarse, heavy and wholly lacking in real ability.

The Jesuit manages the women, which is not a very difficult thing to do, as he holds the leading strings of the sexual life in his hands. In addition he influences the men.

He assists the young who are of good social standing, who belong to distinguished families, and brings about desirable matches. The poor can do anything they like. They are at liberty to eat, to get drunk, to do whatever they will except to read. These unhappy, timid, torpid clerks and hangers-on imagine they are free men whenever they get drunk. They do not see that they are like the Redskins, whom the Yankees poisoned with alcohol so as to hold them in check.

I inspected a club installed in a house in the older part of the city some years ago.

A sign on one door read "Library." When it was opened, I was shown, laughing, a room filled with bottles.

"If a Jesuit could see this, he would be in ecstasy," I exclaimed. "Yes, replacing books with wines and liquors! What a business for the sons of Saint Ignatius!"

In spite of all its display, all its tinsel, all its Jesuitism, all its bad taste, San Sebastian will become an important, dignified city within a very few years. When that time comes, the author who has been born there, will not prefer to hail from some hamlet buried in the mountains, rather than from the capital of Guipúzcoa. But I myself prefer it. I have no city, and I hold myself to be strictly extra-urban.

MY PARENTS

My father, Serafín Baroja y Zornoza, was a mining engineer, who wrote books both in Castilian and Basque, and he, too, came from San Sebastian. My mother's name is Carmen Nessi y Goñi. She was born in Madrid.

I should be a very good man. My father was a good man, although he was capricious and arbitrary, and my mother is a good woman, firmer and more positive in her manifestations of virtue. Yet, I am not without reputation for ferocity, which, perhaps, is deserved.

I do not know why I believed for a long while that I had been born in the Calle del Puyuelo in San Sebastian, where we once lived. The street is well within the old town, and truly ugly and forlorn. The mere idea of it was and is distasteful to me.

When I complained to my mother about my birthplace and its want of attractiveness, she replied that I was born in a beautiful house near the esplanade of La Zurriola, fronting on the Calle de Oquendo, which belonged to my grandmother and looked out upon the sea, although the house does so no longer, as a theatre has been erected directly in front. I am glad that I was born near the sea, because it suggests freedom and change.

My paternal grandmother, Doña Concepción Zornoza, was a woman of positive ideas and somewhat eccentric. She was already old when I knew her. She had mortgaged several houses which she owned in the city in order to build the house which was occupied by us in La Zurriola.

Her plan was to furnish it and rent it to King Amadeo. Before Amadeo arrived at San Sebastian, however, the Carlist war broke out, and the monarch of the house of Savoy was compelled to abdicate, and my grandmother to abandon her plans.

My earliest recollection is the Carlist attempt to bombard San Sebastian. It is a memory which has now grown very dim, and what I saw has been confused with what I have heard. I have a confused recollection of the bringing in of soldiers on stretchers, and of having peeped over the wall of a little cemetery near the city, in which corpses were laid out, still unburied.

As I have said, my father was a mining engineer, but during the war he was engaged in teaching natural history at the Institute. I have no idea how this came about. He was also one of the Liberal volunteers.

I have a vague idea that one night I was taken from my bed, wrapped up in a mantle, and carried to a chalet on the Concha, belonging to one Errazu, who was a relative of my mother's. We lived there for a time in the cellar of the chalet.

Three shells, which were known in those days as cucumbers, dropped on the house, and wrecked the roof, making a great hole in the wall which separated our garden from the next.

MONSIGNOR, THE CAT

Monsignor was a handsome yellow cat belonging to us while we were living in the cellar of Señor Errazu's chalet.

From what I have since learned, his name was a tribute to the extraordinary reputation enjoyed at that period by Monsignor Simeoni.

Monsignor—I am referring to the yellow cat—was intelligent. A bell surmounted the Castillo de la Mota at San Sebastian, by whose side was stationed a look-out. When the look-out spied the flash of Carlist guns, he rang the bell, and then the townspeople retired into the doorways and cellars.

Monsignor was aware of the relation of the bell to the cannonading, so when the bell rang, he promptly withdrew into the house, even going so far sometimes as to creep under the beds.

My father had friends who were not above going down into our cellar on such occasions so as better to observe the manoeuvres of the cat.

TWO LUNATICS

After the war, I used to stroll as a boy with my mother and brothers to the Castillo de la Mota on Sundays. It was truly a beautiful walk, which will soon be ruined utterly by the citizens of San Sebastian. We looked out to sea from the Castillo and then we talked with the guard. We often met a lunatic there, who was in the care of a servant. As soon as he caught sight of us children, the lunatic was happy at once, but if a woman came near him, he ran away and flattened himself against the walls, kicking and crying out: "Blind dog! Blind dog!"

I remember also having seen a young woman, who was insane, in a great house which we used to visit in those days at Loyola. She gesticulated and gazed continually into a deep well, where a half moon of black water was visible far below. These lunatics, one at the Castillo and the other in that great house, haunted my imagination as a child.

THE HAWK

My latest recollection of San Sebastian is of a hawk, which we brought home to our house from the Castillo.

Some soldiers gave us the hawk when it was still very young, and it grew up and became accustomed to living indoors. We fed it snails, which it gulped down as if they were bonbons.

When it was full-grown, it escaped to the courtyard and attacked our chickens, to say nothing of all the cats of the neighbourhood. It hid under the beds during thundershowers.

When we moved away from San Sebastian, we were obliged to leave the hawk behind. We carried him up to the Castillo one day, turned him loose, and off he flew.

IN MADRID

We moved from San Sebastian to Madrid. My father had received an appointment to the Geographic and Political Institute. We lived on the Calle Real, just beyond the Glorieta de Bilbao, in a street which is now a prolongation of the Calle de Fuencarral.

Opposite our house, there was a piece of high ground, which has not yet been removed, which went by the name of "*La Era del Mico*," or "The Monkey Field." Swings and merry-go-rounds were scattered all over it, so that the diversions of "*La Era del Mico*," together with the two-wheeled calashes and chaises which were still in use in those days, and the funerals passing continually through the street, were the amusements which were provided ready-made for us, as we looked down from our balcony.

Two sensational executions took place while we lived here—those of the regicide Otero and of Oliva—one following closely on the heels of the other. We heard the *Salve*, or prayer, which is sung by the prisoners for the criminal awaiting death, hawked about us then on the streets.

IN PAMPLONA

From Madrid we went to Pamplona. Pamplona was still a curious city maintaining customs which would have been appropriate to a state of war. The draw-bridges were raised at night, only one, or perhaps two, gates being left open, I am not certain which.

Pamplona proved an amusing place for a small boy. There were the walls with their glacis, their sentry boxes, their cannon; there were the gates, the river, the cathedral and the surrounding quarters—all of them very attractive to us.

We studied at the Institute and committed all sorts of pranks like the other students. We played practical jokes in the houses of the canons, and threw stones at the bishop's palace, many of the windows of which were already paneless and forlorn.

We also made wild excursions to the roof of our house and to those of other houses in the neighbourhood, prying about the garrets and peering down over the cornices into the courtyards.

Once we seized a stuffed eagle, cherished by a neighbour, hauled it to the attic, pulled it through the skylight to the roof, and flung it down into the street, creating a genuine panic among the innocent passers-by, when they saw the huge bird drop at their feet.

One of my most vivid memories of Pamplona is seeing a criminal on his way to execution passing our house, attired in a round cap and yellow robe.

It was one of the sights which has impressed me most. Later in the afternoon, driven by curiosity, knowing that the man who had been garroted must be still on the scaffold, I ventured alone to see him, and remained there examining him closely for a long time. When I returned home that night, I was unable to sleep because of the impression he had made.

DON TIRSO LAREQUI

Many other vivid memories of Pamplona remain with me, never to be forgotten. I remember a lad of our own age who died, leaping from the wall, and then there were our adventures along the river.

Another terrible memory was associated with the cathedral. I had begun my first year of Latin, and was exactly nine at the time.

We had come out of the Institute, and were watching a funeral. Afterwards, three or four of the boys, among whom were my brother Ricardo and myself, entered the cathedral. The echo of the responses was ringing in my ears and I hummed them, as I wandered about the aisles.

Suddenly, a black shadow shot from behind one of the confessionals, pounced upon me and seized me around the neck with both hands, almost choking me. I was paralyzed with fear. It proved to be a fat, greasy canon, by name Don Tirso Larequi.

"What is your name?" he shouted, shaking me vigorously.

I could not answer because of my fright.

"What is his name?" the priest demanded of the other boys.

"His name is Antonio García," replied my brother Ricardo, coolly.

"Where does he live?"

"In the Calle de Curia, Number 14."

There was no such place, of course.

"I shall see your father at once," shouted the priest, and he rushed out of the cathedral like a bull.

My brother and I then made our escape through the cloister.

This red-faced priest, fat and ferocious, rushing out of the dark to choke a nine-year-old boy, has always been to me a symbol of the Catholic religion.

This experience of my boyhood partly explains my anti-clericalism. I recall Don Tirso with an undying hate, and were he still alive—I have no idea whether he is or not—I should not hesitate to climb up to the roof of his house some dark night, and shout down his chimney in a cavernous voice: "Don Tirso! You are a damned villain!"

A VISIONARY ROWDY

I was something of a rowdy as a boy and rather quarrelsome. The first day I went to school in Pamplona, I came out disputing with another boy of my own age, and we fought in the street until we were separated by a cobbler and the blows of a leather strap, to which he added kicks. Later, I foolishly quarrelled and fought whenever the other boys set me on. In our stone-throwing escapades on the outskirts of the town, I was always the aggressor, and quite indefatigable.

When I began to study medicine, I found that my aggressiveness had departed completely. One day after quarrelling with another student in the cloisters of San Carlos, I challenged him to fight. When we got out on the street, it struck me as foolish to goad him to hit me in the eye or else to land on my nose with his fist, and I slipped off and went home. I lost my morale as a bully then and there. Although I was a fighter from infancy, I was also something of a dreamer, and the two strains scarcely make a harmonious blend.

Before I was grown, I saw Gisbert's Death of the Comuneros reproduced as a chromo. For a long, long while, I always seemed to see that picture hanging in all its variety of colour on the wall before me at night. For months and months after my vigil with the body of the man who had been garroted outside of Pamplona, I never entered a dark room but that his image rose up before me in all its gruesome details. I also passed through a period of disagreeable dreams. Some time would elapse after I awoke before I was able to tell where I was, and I was frightened by it.

SARASATE

It was my opinion then, and still is, that a fiesta at Pamplona is among the most vapid things in the world.

There was a mixture of incomprehension and culture in Pamplona, that was truly ridiculous. The people would devote several days to going to bull fights, and then turn about, when evening came, and welcome Sarasate with Greek fire.

A rude and fanatical populace forgot its orgy of blood to acclaim a violinist. And what a violinist! He was one of the most effeminate and grotesque individuals in the world. I can see him yet, strutting along with his long hair, his ample rear, and his shoes with their little quarter-heels, which gave him the appearance of a fat cook dressed up in men's clothes for Carnival.

When Sarasate died he left a number of trinkets which had been presented to him during his artistic career—mostly match-boxes, cigarette cases, and the like—which the Town Council of Pamplona has assembled and now exhibits in glass cases, but which, in the public interest, should be promptly disposed of at auction.

ROBINSON CRUSOE AND THE MYSTERIOUS ISLAND

During my life in Pamplona, my brother Ricardo imparted his enthusiasm for two stories to me. These were *Robinson Crusoe* and Jules Verne's *The Mysterious Island*, or rather, I should say they were *The Mysterious Island* and *Robinson Crusoe*, because we preferred Jules Verne's tale greatly to Defoe's.

We would dream about desert islands, about manufacturing electric batteries in the fashion of the engineer Cyrus Harding, and as we were not very certain of finding any "Granite House" during the course of our adventures, Ricardo would paint and paint at plans and elevations of houses which we hoped to construct in its place in those far-off, savage lands.

He also made pictures of ships which we took care should be rigged properly.

There were two variations of this dream of adventure—one involving a snow-house, with appropriate episodes such as nocturnal attacks by bears, wolves, and the like, and then we planned a sea voyage.

I rebelled a long time at the notion that my life must be like that of everybody else, but I had no recourse in the end but to capitulate.

IX

AS A STUDENT

I was never more than commonplace as a student, inclining rather to be bad than good. I had no great liking for study, and, to tell the truth, I never entertained any clear idea of what I was studying.

For example, I never knew what the word preterite meant until years after completing my course, although I had repeated over and over again that the preterite, or past perfect, was thus, while the imperfect was thus, without having any conception that the word preterite meant past—that it was a past that was entirely past in the former case, and a past that was past to a less degree in the latter.

To complete two years of Latin grammar, two of French, and one of German without having any conception of what preterite meant, demonstrated one of two things: either my stupidity was very great, or the system of instruction deplorable. Naturally, I incline toward the second alternative.

While preparing to take my degree in medicine, when I was studying chemical analysis, I heard a student, who was already a practising physician, state that zinc was an element which contained a great deal of hydrogen. When the professor attempted to extricate him from his difficulty, it became apparent that the future doctor had no idea of what an element was. My classmate, who doubtless entertained as little liking for chemistry as I did for grammar, had not been able throughout his entire course to grasp the definition of an element, as I had never been able to comprehend what a preterite might be.

For my part—and I believe that all of us have had the same experience—I have never been successful in mastering those subjects which have not interested me.

Doubtless, also, my mental development has been slow.

As for memory, I have always possessed very little. And liking for study, none whatever. Sacred history, or any other history, Latin, French, rhetoric and natural history have interested me not at all. The only subjects for which I cared somewhat, were geometry and physics.

My college course left me with two or three ideas in my head, whereupon I applied myself to making ready for my professional career, as one swallows a bitter dose.

In my novel, *The Tree of Knowledge*, I have drawn a picture of myself, in which the psychological features remain unchanged, although I have altered the hero's environment, as well as his family relations, together with a number of details.

Besides the defects with which I have endowed my hero in this book, I was cursed with an instinctive slothfulness and sluggishness which were not to be denied.

People would tell me: "Now is the time for you to study; later on, you will have leisure to enjoy yourself; and after that will come the time to make money."

But I needed all three times in which to do nothing—and I could have used another three hundred.

PROFESSORS

I have not been fortunate in my professors. It might be urged that I have not been in a position, being idle and sluggish, to take advantage of their instruction. I believe, however, that if they had been good teachers, now that so many years have passed, I should be able to acknowledge their merits.

I cannot remember a single teacher who knew how to teach, or who succeeded in arousing any interest in what he taught, or who had any comprehension of the student mentality. No one learned how to reason in the schools of my youth, nor mastered any theory, nor acquired a practical knowledge of anything. In other words, we learned nothing.

In medicine, the professors adhered to a system that was the most foolish imaginable. In the two universities in which I studied, subjects might be taken only by halves, which would have been ridiculous enough in any branch, but it was even more preposterous in medicine. Thus, in pathology, a certain number of intending physicians studied the subject of infection, while others studied nervous disorders, and yet others the diseases of the respiratory organs. Nobody studied all three. A plan of this sort could only have been conceived by Spanish professors, who, it may be said in general, are the quintessence of vacuity.

"What difference does it make whether the students learn anything or not?" every Spanish professor asks himself continually.

Unamuno says, apropos of the backwardness of Spaniards in the field of invention: "Other nations can do the inventing." In other words, let foreigners build up the sciences, so that we may take advantage of them.

There was one among my professors who considered himself a born teacher and, moreover, a man of genius, and he was Letamendi. I made clear in my *Tree of Knowledge* what I thought of this professor, who was not destitute, indeed, of a certain talent as an orator and man of letters. When he wrote, he was rococo, like so many Catalans. Sometimes he would discourse upon art, especially upon painting, in the class-room, but the ideas he entertained were preposterous. I recall that he once said that a mouse and a book were not a fit subject for a painting, but if you were to write the words *Aristotle's Works* on the book, and then set the mouse to gnawing at it, what had originally meant nothing would immediately become a subject for a picture. Yes, a picture to be hawked at the street fairs!

Letamendi was prolixity and puerile ingenuity personified. Yet Letamendi was no different from all other Spaniards of his day, including even the most celebrated, such as Castelar, Echegaray and Valera.

These men read much, they possessed good memories, but I verily believe that, honestly, they understood nothing. Not one of them had an inkling of that almost tragic sense of the dignity of culture or of the obligations which it imposes, which distinguishes the Germans above all other nationalities. They nearly all revealed an attitude toward science which would have sat easily upon a smart, sharp-tongued Andalusian young gentleman.

I recall a profoundly moving letter by the critic Garve, which is included in Kant's *Prolegomena*.

Garve wrote an article upon *The Critique of Pure Reason*, and sent it to a journal at Göttingen, and the editor of the journal, in malice and animosity toward Kant, so altered it that it became an attack on the philosopher, and then published it unsigned.

Kant invited his anonymous critic to divulge his name, whereupon Garve wrote to Kant explaining what had taken place, and Kant made a reply.

It would be difficult to parallel in nobility these two letters, which were exchanged between a comprehensive intellect such as Garve and one of the most portentous geniuses of the world, as was Kant.

They appear to be two travellers, face to face with the mystery of Nature and the Unknown. No such feeling for learning and culture is to be met with among our miserably affected Latin mountebanks.

ANTI-MILITARISM

I am an anti-militarist by inheritance. The Basques have never been good soldiers in the regular army. My great-grandfather Nessi probably fled from Italy as a deserter. I have always loathed barracks, messes, and officers profoundly.

One day, when I was studying therapeutics with Don Benito Hernando, my brother opened the door of the class-room and motioned for me to come out.

I did so, at the cost, by the way, of a furious scene with Don Benito, who shattered several test tubes in his wrath.

The cause of my brother's appearance was to advise me that the Alcaldía del Centro, or Town Council of the Central District, had given notice to the effect that if I did not present myself for the draft, I was to be declared in default. As I had already laid before the Board a copy of a royal decree in which my name was set down as exempt from the draft because my father had served as a Liberal Volunteer in the late war, and because, in addition, I was born in the Basque provinces, I had supposed that the matter had been disposed of. One of those ill-natured, dictatorial officials who held sway in the offices of the Board, took it upon himself to rule that the exemption held good only in the Basque provinces, but not in Madrid, and so, in fact, for the time it proved to be. In spite of my furious protests, I was compelled to report and submit to have my measurements taken, and was well nigh upon the point of being marched off to the barracks.

"I am no soldier," I thought to myself. "If they insist, I shall run away."

I went at once from the Alcaldía to the Ministry and called upon a Guipúzcoan politician, as my father had previously advised me to do; but the man was a political mastodon, puffed up with huge pretensions, who, perhaps, might have been a stevedore in any other country. So he did nothing. Finally, it occurred to me to go and see the Conde de Romanones, who had just been appointed Alcalde del Centro, having jurisdiction over the district.

When I entered his office, Romanones appeared to be in a jovial frame of mind. He wore a flower in his button-hole. Two persons were with him, one of whom was no other than the Secretary of the Board, my enemy.

I related what had happened to Romanones with great force. The Secretary then answered.

"The young man is right," said the Count. "Bring me the roll of the draft."

The roll was brought. Romanones took his pen and crossed my name off altogether. Then he turned to me with a smile:

"Don't you care to be a soldier?"

"No, sir."

"But what are you, a student?"

"Yes, sir."

"In which branch?"

"Medicine."

"Good! Very good. You may go now."

I would willingly have been anything to have escaped becoming a soldier, and so be obliged to live in barracks, eat mess, and parade.

TO VALENCIA

I failed in both June and September during the fourth year of my course, which was a mere matter of luck, as I neither applied myself more nor less than in previous years.

In the meantime my father had been transferred to Valencia, whither it seemed wise that I should remove to continue my studies.

I appeared at Valencia in January for a second examination in general pathology, and failed for the second time.

I began to consider giving up my intended profession.

I found that I had lost what little liking I had for it. As I had no friends in Valencia, I never left the house; I had nowhere to go. I passed my days stretched out on the roof, or, else, in reading. After debating long what I should do, and realizing fully that there was no one obvious plan to pursue, I determined to finish my course, committing the required subjects mechanically. After adopting this plan, I never failed once.

When I came up for graduation, the professors made an effort to put some obstacles in my way, which, however, were not sufficient to detain me.

Admitted as a physician, I decided next to study for the doctor's degree at Madrid.

My former fellow-students, when they saw that now I was doing nicely, all exclaimed:

"How you have changed! Now you pass your examinations."

"Passing examinations, you know, is a combination, like a gambling game," I told them.

"I have found a combination."

X

AS A VILLAGE DOCTOR

I returned to Burjasot, a small town near Valencia, where my family lived at the time, a full-fledged doctor. We had a tiny house, besides a garden containing pear, peach and pomegranate trees.

I passed some time there very pleasantly.

My father was a contributor to the *Voz de Guipúzcoa* of San Sebastian, so he always received the paper. One day I read—or it may have been one of the family—that the post of official physician was vacant in the town of Cestona.

I decided to apply for the place, and dispatched a letter accompanied by a copy of my diploma. It turned out that I was the only applicant, and so the post was awarded to me.

I set out for Madrid, where I passed the night, and then proceeded to San Sebastian, receiving a letter from my father upon my arrival, informing me that there was another physician at Cestona who was receiving a larger salary than that which had been offered to me, and recommending that perhaps it would be better not to put in appearance too soon, until I was better advised as to the prospects.

I hesitated.

"In any event," I thought, "I shall learn what the town is like. If I like it, I shall stay; if not, I shall return to Burjasot."

I took the diligence, which goes by the name of "La Vascongada," and made the trip from San Sebastian to Cestona, which proved to be long enough in all conscience, as we were five or six hours late. I got off at a posada, or small inn, at Alcorta, to get something to eat. I dined sumptuously, drank bravely, and, encouraged by the good food, made up my mind to remain in the village. I talked with the other doctor and with the alcalde, and soon everything was arranged that had to be arranged.

As night was coming on, the priest and the doctor recommended that I go to board at the house of the Sacristana, as she had a room vacant, which had formerly been occupied by a notary.

DOLORES, LA SACRISTANA

Dolores, my landlady and mistress of the Sacristy, was an agreeable, exceedingly energetic, exceedingly hard-working woman, who was a pronounced conservative.

I have met few women as good as she. In spite of the fact that she soon discovered that I was not at all religious, she did not hold it against me, nor did I harbour any resentment against her.

I often read her the *Añalejo*, or church calendar, which is known as the *Gallofa*, or beggars' mite, in the northern provinces, in allusion to the ancient custom of making pilgrimages to Santiago, and I cooked sugar wafers over the fire with her on the eve of feast days, at which times her work was especially severe.

I realized in Cestona my childish ambitions of having a house of my own, and a dog, which had lain in my mind ever since reading *Robinson Crusoe* and *The Mysterious Island*.

I also had an old horse named Juanillo, which I borrowed from a coachman in San Sebastian, but I never liked horses.

The horse seems to me to be a militaristic, antipathetic animal. Neither Robinson Crusoe nor Cyrus Harding rode horse-back.

I committed no blunders while I was a village doctor. I had already grown prudent, and my sceptical temperament was a bar to any great mistakes.

I first began to realize that I was a Basque in Cestona, and I recovered my pride of race there, which I had lost.

XI

AS A BAKER

I have been asked frequently: "How did you ever come to go into the baking business?" I shall now proceed to answer the question, although the story is a long one.

My mother had an aunt, Juana Nessi, who was a sister of her father's.

This lady was reasonably attractive when young, and married a rich gentleman just returned from America, whose name was Don Matías Lacasa.

Once settled in Madrid, Don Matías, who deemed himself an eagle, when, in reality, he was a common barnyard rooster, embarked upon a series of undertakings that failed with truly extraordinary unanimity. About 1870, a physician from Valencia by the name of Martí, who had visited Vienna, gave him an account of the bread they make there, and of the yeast they use to raise it, enlarging upon the profits which lay ready to hand in that line.

Don Matías was convinced, and he bought an old house near the Church of the Descalzas upon Martí's advice. It stood in a street which boasted only one number—the number 2. I believe the street was, and still is, called the Calle de la Misericordia.

Martí set up ovens in the old building by the Church of the Descalzas, and the business began to yield fabulous profits. Being a devotee of the life of pleasure, Martí died three or four years after the business had been established, and Don Matías continued his gallinaceous evolutions until he was utterly ruined, and had pawned everything he possessed, remaining at last with the bakery as his only means of support.

He succeeded in entangling and ruining that, too, before he died. My aunt then wrote my mother requesting that my brother Ricardo come up to Madrid.

My brother remained in Madrid for some time, when he grew tired and left; then I went, and later we were both there together, making an effort to improve the business and to push it ahead. Times were bad: there was no way of pushing ahead. Surely the proverb "Where flour is lacking, everything goes packing," could never have been applied with more truth. And we could get no flour.

When the bakery was just about to do better, the Conde de Romanones, who was our landlord in those days, notified us that the building was to be torn down.

Then our troubles began. We were obliged to move elsewhere, and to undertake alterations, for which money was indispensable, but we had no money. In that predicament, we began to speculate upon the Exchange, and the Exchange proved a kind mother to us; it sustained us until we were on our feet again. As soon as we had established ourselves upon another site, we proceeded to lose money, so we withdrew.

It is not surprising, therefore, that I have always regarded the Stock Exchange as a philanthropic institution, or that, on the other hand, a church has always seemed a sombre place in which a black priest leaps forth from behind a confessional to seize one by the throat in the dark, and to throttle him.

MY FATHER'S DISILLUSIONMENT

My father was endowed with a due share of the romantic fervour which distinguished men of his epoch, and set great store by friendship. More particularly, he was wrapped up in his friends in San Sebastian.

When we discovered that we were in trouble, before throwing ourselves into the loving arms of the Bourse, my father spoke to two intimate friends of his who were from San Sebastian. They made an appointment to meet me in the Café Suizo. I explained the situation to them, after which they made me certain propositions, which were so usurious, so outrageously extortionate, that they took my breath away. They offered to advance us the money we needed for fifty per cent of the gross receipts, while we were to meet the running expenses out of our fifty per cent, receiving no compensation whatever for our services in taking care of the business.

I was astonished, and naturally did not accept. The episode was a great blow to my father. I frequently came face to face with one of our friends at a later date, but I never bowed to him. He was offended. I was tempted to approach him and say: "The reason that I do not bow to you is because I know you are a rascal."

If either of these friends of ours were alive, I should proceed to mention their names, but, as they are dead, it will serve no useful purpose.

INDUSTRY AND DEMOCRACY

The bakery has been brandished against me in literature.

When I first wrote, it was said:

"This Baroja is a crusty fellow; naturally, he is a baker."

A certain picturesque academician, who was also a dramatist, and given to composing stupendous *quintillas* and *cuartetas* in his day, which, despite their flatness, were received with applause, had the inspiration to add:

"All this modernism has been cooked up in Baroja's oven."

Even the Catalans lost no time in throwing the fact of my being a baker in my face, although they are a commercial, manufacturing people. Whether calico is nobler than flour, or flour than calico, I am not sure, but the subject is one for discussion, as Maeztu would have it.

I am an eclectic myself on this score. I prefer flour in the shape of bread with my dinner, but cloth will go further with a man who desires to appear well in public.

When I was serving upon the Town Council, an anonymous publication entitled "Masks Off," printed the following among other gems: "Pío Baroja is a man of letters who runs a bake-shop."

A Madrid critic recently declared in an American periodical that I had two personalities: one that of a writer and the other of a baker. He was solicitous to let me know later that he intended no harm.

But if I should say to him: "Mr. So and So" is a writer who is excellently posted upon the value of cloth, as his father sold dry-goods, it would appeal to his mind as bad taste.

Another journalist paid his respects to me some months ago in *El Parlamentario*, saying I baked rolls, oppressed the people, and sucked the blood of the workingman.

It would appear to be more demeaning to own a small factory or a shop, according to the standards of both literary and non-literary circles, than it is to accept money from the corruption funds of the Government, or bounties from the exchequers of foreign Embassies.

When I hear talk nowadays about the dues of the common people, my propensity to laugh is so great that I am apprehensive that my end may be like that of the Greek philosopher in Diogenes Laertius, who died of laughter because he saw an ass eating figs.

THE VEXATIONS OF A SMALL TRADESMAN

The trials and tribulations of the literary life, its feuds and its backbitings are a common topic of conversation. However, I have never experienced anything of the kind in literature. The trouble with literature is that there is very little money in it, which renders the writer's existence both mean and precarious.

Nothing compares for vexation with the life of the petty tradesman, especially when that tradesman is a baker. Upon occasion, I have repeated to my friends the series of outrages to which we were obliged to submit, in particular at the hands of the municipal authorities.

Sometimes it was through malice, but more often through sheer insentient imbecility.

When my brother and I moved to the new site, we drew up a plan and submitted it to the *Ayuntamiento*, or City Government. A clerk discovered that no provision had been made for a stall for a mule to run the kneading machine, and so rejected it. When we learned that our application had not been granted, we inquired the reason and explained to the clerk that no provision had been made for the mule because we had no mule, as our kneading machine was operated by an electric motor.

"That makes no difference, no difference whatever," replied the clerk with the importance and obtuseness of the bureaucrat. "The ordinance requires that there be a stall for one."

Another of the thousand instances of official barbarity was perpetrated at our expense while Sánchez de Toca was Alcalde. This gentleman is a Siamese twin of Maura's when it comes to garrulousness and muddy thinking, and he had resolved to do away with the distribution of bread by public delivery, and to license only deliveries by private bakeries. The order was arbitrary enough, but the manner in which it was put into effect was a masterpiece. It was reported that plates bearing license numbers would be given out at the *Ayuntamiento* to the delivery men from the bakeries. So we repaired to the *Ayuntamiento* and questioned a clerk:

"Where do they give out the numbers?"

"There are no numbers."

"What will happen tomorrow then, when we make our deliveries?"

"How do I know?"

The next day when the delivery men began their rounds, a policeman accosted them:

"Have you your numbers?"

"No, sir; they are not ready yet."

"Well, come with me then, to the police station."

And that was the last of our bread.

The Caid of Mechuar in Morocco favoured his subjects in some such fashion several years since, but the Moors, being men of spirit, fell on him one day, and left him at death's door on a dung heap. Meanwhile, Sánchez de Toca continues to talk nonsense in these parts, and is considered by some to be one of the bulwarks of the country.

I could spin many a tale of tyranny in high places, and almost as many, no doubt, of the pettinesses of workingmen. But what is the good? Why stir up my bile? In progressive incarnations, I have now passed through those of baker and petty tradesman. I am no longer an employer who exploits the workingman, nor can I see that I ever did so. If I have exploited workers merely because I employed them, all that was some time ago. I support myself by my writings now, although it is quite proper to state that I live on very little.

XII

AS A WRITER

My pre-literary career was three-fold: I was a student for eight years, during two a village doctor, and for six more a baker.

These having elapsed, being already close upon thirty, I began to write.

My new course was a wise one. It was the best thing that I could have done; anything else would have annoyed me more and have pleased me less. I have enjoyed writing, and I have made some money, although not much, yet it has been sufficient to enable me to travel, which otherwise I should not have been able to do.

The first considerable sum which I received was upon the publication of my novel *The Mayorazgo of Labraz*. Henrich of Barcelona paid me two thousand pesetas for it. I invested the two thousand pesetas in a speculation upon the Bourse, and they disappeared in two weeks.

The money which I have received for my other books, I have employed to better purpose.

BOHEMIA

I have never been a believer in the absurd myth called Bohemia. The idea of living gaily and irresponsibly in Madrid, or in any other Spanish city, without taking thought for the morrow, is so preposterous that it passes comprehension. Bohemia is utterly false in Paris and London, but in Spain, where life is difficult, it is even more of a cheat.

Bohemia is not only false, it is contemptible. It suggests to me a minor Christian sect, of the most inconsequential degree, nicely calculated for the convenience of hangers on at cafés.

Henri Murger was the son of the wife of a *concièrge*.

Of course, this would not have mattered had his outlook upon life not been that of the son of the wife of a *concièrge*.

OUR OWN GENERATION

The beginner in letters makes his way up, as a rule, amid a literary environment which is distinguished by reputations and hierarchies, all respected by him. But this was not the case with the young writers of my day. During the years 1898 to 1900, a number of young men suddenly found themselves thrown together in Madrid, whose only rule was the principle that the immediate past did not exist for them.

This aggregation of authors and artists might have seemed to have been brought together under some leadership, and to have been directed to some purpose; yet one who entertained such an assumption would have been mistaken.

Chance brought us together for a moment, a very brief moment, to be followed by a general dispersal. There were days when thirty or forty young men, apprentices in the art of writing, sat around the tables in the old Café de Madrid.

Doubtless such gatherings of new men, eager to interfere in and to influence the operations of the social system, yet without either the warrant of tradition or any proved ability to do so, are common upon a larger scale in all revolutions.

As we neither had, nor could have had, in the nature of the case, a task to perform, we soon found that we were divided into small groups, and finally broke up altogether.

AZORÍN

A few days after the publication of my first book, *Sombre Lives*, Miguel Poveda, who was responsible for printing it, sent a copy to Martínez Ruiz, who was at that time in Monóvar. Martínez Ruiz wrote me a long letter concerning the book by return mail; on the following day he sent another.

Poveda handed me the letters to read and I was filled with surprise and joy. Some weeks later, returning from the National Library, Martínez Ruiz, whom I knew by sight, came up to me on the Recoletos.

"Are you Baroja?" he asked.

"Yes."

"I am Martínez Ruiz."

We shook hands and became friends.

In those days we travelled about the country together, we contributed to the same papers, and the ideas and the men we attacked were the same.

Later, Azorín became an enthusiastic partisan of Maura, which appeared to me particularly absurd, as I have never been able to see anything but an actor of the grand style in Maura, a man of small ideas. Next he became a partisan of La Cierva, which was as bad in my opinion as being a Maurista. I am unable to say at the moment whether he is contemplating any further transformations.

But, whether he is or not, Azorín will always remain a master of language to me, besides an excellent friend who has a weakness for believing all men to be great who talk in a loud voice and who pull their cuffs down out of their coat sleeves with a grand gesture whenever they appear upon the platform.

PAUL SCHMITZ

Another friendship which I found stimulating was that of Paul Schmitz, a Swiss from Basle, who had come to Madrid because of some weakness of the lungs, spending three years among us in order to rehabilitate himself. Schmitz had studied in Switzerland and in Germany, and also had lived for a long time in the north of Russia.

He was familiar with what in my judgment are the two most interesting countries of Europe.

Paul Schmitz was a timid person of an inquiring turn of mind, whose youth had been tempestuous. I made a number of excursions with Schmitz to Toledo, to El Paular and to the Springs of Urbión; a year or two later we visited Switzerland several times together.

Schmitz was like an open window through which I looked out upon an unknown world. I held long conversations with him upon life, literature, art and philosophy.

I recall that I took him one Sunday afternoon to the home of Don Juan Valera.

When Schmitz and I arrived, Valera had just settled down for the afternoon to listen to his daughter, who was reading aloud one of the latest novels of Zola.

Valera, Schmitz and I sat chatting for perhaps four or five hours. There was no subject that we could all agree upon. Valera and I were no sooner against the Swiss than the Swiss and Valera were against me, or the Swiss and I against Valera, and then each flew off after his own opinion.

Valera, who saw that the Swiss and I were anarchists, said it was beyond his comprehension how any man could conceive of a state of general well being.

"Do you mean to say that you believe," he said to me, "that there will ever come a time when every man will be able to set a bowl of oysters from Arcachón upon his table and top it off with a bottle of champagne of first-rate vintage, besides having a woman sitting beside him in a Worth gown?"

"No, no, Don Juan," I replied. "In the eyes of the anarchist, oysters, champagne, and Worth are mere superstitions, myths to which we attach no importance. We do not spend our time dreaming about oysters, while champagne is not nectar to our tastes. All that we ask is to live well, and to have those about us live well also."

We could not convince each other. When Schmitz and I left Valera's house it was already night, and we found ourselves absorbed in his talents and his limitations.

ORTEGA Y GASSET

Ortega y Gasset impresses me as a traveller who has journeyed through the world of culture. He moves upon a higher level, which it is difficult to reach, and upon which it is still more difficult to maintain oneself.

It may be that Ortega has no great sympathy for my manner of living, which is insubordinate; it may be that I look with unfriendly eye upon his ambitious and aristocratic sympathies; nevertheless, he is a master who brings glad news of the unknown—that is, of the unknown to us.

Doctor San Martín was fond of telling how he was sitting one day upon a bench in the Retiro, reading.

"Are you reading a novel?" inquired a gentleman, sitting down beside him.

"No, I am studying."

"What! Studying at your age?" exclaimed the gentleman, amazed.

The same remark might be made to me: "What! Sitting under a master at your age?"

As far as I am concerned, every man who knows more than I do is my master.

I know very well that philosophy and metaphysics are nothing to the great mass of physicians who pick up their science out of foreign reviews, adding nothing themselves to what they read; nor, for that matter, are they to most Spanish engineers, who are skilled in doing sufficiently badly today what was done in England and Germany very well thirty years ago; and the same thing is true of the apothecaries. The practical is all that these people concede to exist, but how do they know what is practical? Considering the matter from the practical point of view, there can be no doubt but that civilization has attained a high development wherever there have been great metaphysicisms, and then with the philosophers have come the inventors, who between them are the glory of mankind. Unamuno despises inventors, but in this case it is his misfortune. It is far easier for a nation which is destitute of a tradition of culture to improvise an histologist or a physicist, than a philosopher or a real thinker.

Ortega y Gasset, the only approach to a philosopher whom I have ever known, is one of the few Spaniards whom it is interesting to hear talk.

A PSEUDO-PATRON

Although a man may never have amounted to anything, and will probably continue in much the same case, that is to say never amounting to anything, yet there are persons who will take pride in having given him his start in the world—in short, upon having made him known. Señor Ruiz Contreras has set up some such absurd claim in regard to me. According to Ruiz Contreras, he brought me into public notice through a review which he published in 1899, under the title *Revista Nueva*. Thus, according to Ruiz Contreras, I am known, and have been for eighteen years! Although it may seem scarcely worth while to expose such an obvious joke, I should like to clear up this question for the benefit of any future biographers. Why should I not indulge the hope of having them?

In 1899, Ruiz Contreras invited my co-operation in a weekly magazine, in which I was to be both stockholder and editor. Those days already seem a long way off. At first I refused, but he insisted; at length we agreed that I should write for the magazine and share in meeting the expenses, in company with Ruiz Contreras, Reparaz, Lassalle and the novelist Matheu.

I made two or three payments, and moved down some of my pictures and furniture to the office in consequence, until the time came when I began to feel that it was humorous for me to be paying for publishing my articles, when I was perfectly well able to dispose of them to any other sheet. Upon my cutting off payments, Ruiz Contreras informed me that a number of the stockholders, among whom was Icaza, who had replaced Reparaz, took the position that if I did not pay, I should not be permitted to write for the magazine.

"Very well, I shall not write." And I ceased to write.

Previous to my connection with the *Revista Nueva*, I had contributed articles to *El Liberal*, *El Pais*, *El Globo*, *La Justicia*, and *La Voz de Guipúzcoa*, as well as to other publications.

A year after my contributions to the *Revista Nueva*, I brought out *Sombre Lives*, which scarcely sold one hundred copies, and, then, a little later, *The House of Aizgorri*, the sale of which fell short of fifty.

At this time, Martínez Ruiz published a comedy, *The Power of Love*, for which I provided a prologue, and I went about with the publisher, Rodríguez Serra, through the bookshops, peddling the book. In a shop on the Plaza de Santa Ana, Rodríguez Serra asked the proprietor, not altogether without a touch of malice:

"What do you think of this book?"

"It would be all right," answered the proprietor, who did not know me, "if anybody knew who Martínez Ruiz was; and who is this Pío Baroja?"

Señor Ruiz Contreras says that he made me known, but the fact is that nobody knew me in those days; Señor Ruiz Contreras flatters himself that he did me a great favour by publishing my articles, at a cost to me, at the very least, of two or three *duros* apiece.

If this is to be a patron of letters, I should like to patronize half the planet.

As for literary influence, Ruiz Contreras never had any upon me. He was an admirer of Arsène Houssage, Paul Bourget, and other novelists with a sophisticated air, who never meant anything to me. The theatre also obsessed him, a malady which I have never suffered, and he was a devotee of the poet, Zorrilla, in which respect I was unable to share his enthusiasm, nor can I do so today. Finally, he was a political reactionary, while I am a man of radical tendencies.

XIII

PARISIAN DAYS

For the past twenty years I have been in the habit of visiting Paris, not for the purpose of becoming acquainted with the city—to see it once is enough; nor do I go in order to meet French authors, as, for the most part, they consider themselves so immeasurably above Spaniards that there is no way in which a self-respecting person can approach them. I go to meet the members of the Spanish colony, which includes some types which are most interesting.

I have gathered a large number of stories and anecdotes in this way, some of which I have incorporated in my books.

ESTÉVANEZ

Don Nicolás Estévanez was a good friend of mine. During my sojourns in Paris, I met him every afternoon in the Café de la Fleur in the Boulevard St. Germain.

When I was writing *The Last of the Romantics* and *Grotesque Tragedies*, Estévanez furnished me with data and information concerning life in Paris under the Second Empire.

When I last saw him in the autumn of 1913, he made a practice of coming to the café with a paper scribbled over with notes, to assist his memory to recall the anecdotes which he had it in mind to tell.

I can see him now in the Café de la Fleur, with his blue eyes, his long white beard, his cheeks, which were still rosy, his calm and always phlegmatic air.

Once he became much excited. Javier Bueno and I happened on him in a café on the Avenue d'Orleans, not far from the Lion de Belfort. Bueno asked some questions about the recent attempt by Moral to assassinate the King in Madrid, and Estévanez suddenly went to pieces. An anarchist told me afterwards that Estévanez had carried the bomb which was thrown by Morral in Madrid, from Paris to Barcelona, at which port he had taken ship for Cuba, by arrangement with the Duke of Bivona.

I believe this story to have been a pure fabrication, but I feel perfectly certain that Estévanez knew beforehand that the crime was to be attempted.

MY VERSATILITY ACCORDING TO BONAFOUX

Speaking of Estévanez, I recall also Bonafoux, whom I saw frequently. According to González de la Peña, the painter, he held my versatility against me.

"Bonafoux," remarked Peña, "feels that you are too versatile and too volatile."

"Indeed? In what way?"

"One day you entered the bar and said to Bonafoux that a testimonial banquet ought to be organized for Estévanez, enlarging upon it enthusiastically. Bonafoux answered: 'Go ahead and make the preparations, and we will all get together.' When you came into the café a few nights later, Bonafoux asked: 'How about that banquet?' 'What banquet?' you replied. It had already passed out of your mind. Now, tell me: Is this true?" inquired Peña.

"Yes, it is. We all have something of Tartarin in us, more or less. We talk and we talk, and then we forget what we say."

Other Parisian types return to me when I think of those days. There was a Cuban journalist, who was satisfactorily dirty, of whom Bonafoux used to say that he not only ate his plate of soup but managed to wash his face in it at the same time. There was a Catalan guitar player, besides some girls from Madrid who walked the tight rope, whom we used to invite to join us at the café from time to time. And then there was a whole host of other persons, all more or less shabby, down at the heel and picturesque.

XIV

LITERARY ENMITIES

Making our entrance into the world of letters hurling contradictions right and left, the young men of our generation were received by the writers of established reputation with unfriendly demonstrations. As was natural, this was not only the attitude of the older writers, but it extended to our contemporaries in years as well, even to those who were most modern.

THE ENMITY OF DICENTA

Among those who cherished a deadly hatred of me was Dicenta. It was an antipathy which had its origin in the realm of ideas, and it was accentuated subsequently by an article which I contributed to *El Globo* upon his drama *Aurora*, in which I maintained that Dicenta was not a man of new or broad ideas, but completely preoccupied with the ancient conceptions of honesty and honour. One night in the Café Fornos—I am able to vouch for the truth of this incident because, years afterwards, he told me the story himself—Dicenta accosted a young man who was sitting at an adjacent table taking supper, and attempted to draw him into discussion, under the impression that it was I. The young man was so frightened that he never dared to open his mouth.

"Come," shouted Dicenta, "we shall settle this matter at once."

"I have nothing to settle with you," replied the young man.

"Yes, sir, you have; you have stated in an article that my ideas are not revolutionary."

"I never stated anything of the kind."

"What is that?"

"No, sir."

"But aren't you Pío Baroja?"

"I am not, sir."

Dicenta turned on his heel and marched back to his seat.

Sometime later, Dicenta and I became friends, although we were never very intimate, because he felt that I did not appreciate him at his full worth. And it was the truth.

THE POSTHUMOUS ENMITY OF SAWA

I met Alejandro Sawa one evening at the Café Fornos, where I had gone with a friend.

As a matter of fact, I had never read anything which he had written, but his appearance impressed me. Once I followed him in the street with the intention of speaking to him, but my courage failed at the last moment. A number of months later, I met him one summer afternoon on the Recoletos, when he was in the company of a Frenchman named Cornuty. Cornuty and Sawa were conversing and reciting verses; they took me to a wine-shop in the Plaza de Herradores, where they drank a number of glasses, which I paid for, whereupon Sawa asked me to lend him three pesetas. I did not have them, and told him so.

"Do you live far from here?" asked Alejandro, in his lofty style.

"No, near by."

"Very well then, you can go home and bring me the money."

He issued this command with such an air of authority that I went home and brought him the money. He came to the door of the wine-shop, took it from me, and then said:

"You may go now."

This was the way in which insignificant bourgeois admirers were treated in the school of Baudelaire and Verlaine.

Later again, when I brought out *Sombre Lives*, I sometimes saw Sawa in the small hours of the morning, his long locks flowing, and followed by his dog. He always gripped my hand with such force that it did me some hurt, and then he would say to me, in a tragic tone:

"Be proud! You have written *Sombre Lives*."

I took it as a joke.

One day Alejandro wrote me to come to his house. He was living on the Cuesta de Santo Domingo. I betook myself there, and he made me a proposition which was obviously preposterous. He handed me five or six articles, written by him, which had already been published, together with some notes, saying that if I would add certain material, we should then be able to make up a book of "Parisian Impressions," which could appear under the names of us both.

I read the articles and did not care for them. When I went to return them, he asked me:

"What have you done?"

"Nothing. I think it would be difficult for us to collaborate; there is no possible bond of unity in what we write."

"How is that?"

"You are one of these eloquent writers, and I am not."

This remark gave great offence.

Another reason for Alejandro's enmity was an opinion expressed by my brother, Ricardo.

Ricardo wished to paint the portrait of Manuel Sawa in oils, as Manuel had marked personality at that time, when he still wore a beard.

"But here am I," said Alejandro. "Am I not a more interesting subject to be painted?"

"No, no, not at all," we all shouted together—this took place in the Café de Lisboa—"Manuel has more character."

Alejandro said nothing, but, a few moments later, he rose, looked at himself in the glass, arranged his flowing locks, and then, glaring at us from top to toe, while he pronounced the letter with the utmost distinctness, he said simply:

"M...." and walked out of the café.

Some time passed before Alejandro heard that I had put him into one of my novels and he conceived a certain dislike for me, in spite of which we saw each other now and then, always conversing affectionately.

One day he sent for me to come and see him. He was living in the Calle del Conde Duque. He was in bed, already blind. His spirit was as high as before, while his interest in literary matters remained the same. His brother, Miguel, who was present, happened to say during the conversation that the hat I wore, which I had purchased in Paris a few days previously, had a flatter brim than was usual. Alejandro asked to examine it, and busied himself feeling of the brim.

"This is a hat," he exclaimed enthusiastically, "that a man can wear with long hair." Some months subsequent to his death a book of his, *Light Among the Shadows*, was published, in which Alejandro spoke ill of me, although he had a good word for *Sombre Lives*.

He called me a country-man, said that my bones were misshapen, and then stated that glory does not go hand in hand with tuberculosis. Poor Alejandro! He was sound at heart, an eloquent child of the Mediterranean, born to orate in the lands of the sun, but he took it into his head that it was his duty to make himself over into the likeness of one of the putrid products of the North.

SEMI-HATRED ON THE PART OF SILVERIO LANZA

A mutual friend, Antonio Gil Campos, introduced me to Silverio Lanza.

Silverio Lanza was a man of great originality, endowed with an enormous fund of thwarted ambition and pride, which was only natural, as he was a notably fine writer who had not yet met with success, nor even with the recognition which other younger writers enjoyed.

The first time that I saw Lanza, I remember how his eyes sparkled when I told him that I liked his books. Nobody ever paid any attention to him in those days.

Silverio Lanza was a singular character. At times he seemed benevolent, and then again there were times when he would appear malignant in the extreme.

His ideas upon the subject of literature were positively absurd. When I sent him *Sombre Lives*, he wrote me an unending letter in which he attempted to convince me that I ought to append a lesson or moral, to every tale. If I did not wish to write them, he offered to do it himself.

Silverio thought that literature was not to be composed like history, according to Quintilian's definition, *ad narrandum*, but *ad probandum*.

When I gave him *The House of Aizgorri*, he was outraged by the optimistic conclusion of the book, and advised me to change it. According to his theory, if the son of the Aizgorri family came to a bad end, the daughter ought to come to a bad end also.

Being of a somewhat fantastical turn of mind, Silverio Lanza was full of political projects that were extraordinary.

I remember that one of his ideas was that we ought all to write the King a personal note of congratulation upon his attaining his majority.

"It is the most revolutionary thing that can be done at such a time," insisted Lanza, apparently quite convinced.

"I am unable to see it," I replied. Azorín and myself were of the opinion that it was a ridiculous proceeding which would never produce the desired result.

Another of Lanza's hobbies was an aggressive misogyny.

"Baroja, my friend," he would say to me, "you are too gallant and respectful in your novels with the ladies. Women are like laws, they are to be violated."

I laughed at him.

One day I was walking with my friend Gil Campos and my cousin Goñi, when we happened on Silverio Lanza, who took us to the Café de San Sebastián, where we sat down in the section facing the Plazuela del Angel. It was a company that was singularly assorted.

Silverio reverted to the theme that women should be handled with the rod. Gil Campos proceeded to laugh, being gifted with an ironic vein, and made fun of him. For my part, I was tired of it, so I said to Lanza:

"See here, Don Juan" (his real name was Juan Bautista Amorós), "what you are giving us now is literature, and poor literature at that. You are not, and I am not, able to violate law and women as we see fit. That may be all very well for Caesars and Napoleons and Borgias, but you are a respectable gentleman who lives in a little house at Getafe with your wife, and I am a poor man myself, who manages as best he may to make a living. You would tremble in your boots if you ever broke a law, or even a municipal ordinance, and so would I. As far as women are concerned, we are both of us glad to take what we can get, if we can get anything, and I am afraid that neither of us is ever going to get very much, despite the fact"—I added by way of a humorous touch—"that we are two of the most distinguished minds in Europe."

My cousin Goñi replied to this with the rare tact that was characteristic of him, arguing that within the miserable sphere of tangible reality I was right, while Lanza moved upon a higher plane, which was more ideal and more romantic. He went on to add that Lanza and he were both Berbers, and so violent and passionate, while I was an Aryan, although a vulgar Aryan, whose ideas were simply those which were shared by everybody.

Lanza was not satisfied with my cousin's explanation and departed with a marked lack of cordiality.

Since that time, Silverio has regarded me with mixed emotions, half friendly, half the reverse, although in one of his latest books, *The Surrender of Santiago*, he has referred to me as a great friend and a great writer. I suspect, however, that he does not love me.

XV

THE PRESS

OUR NEWSPAPERS AND PERIODICALS

I have always been very much interested in the newspaper and periodical press, and in everything that has any connection with printing. When my father, my grandfather, and great grandfather set up struggling papers in a provincial capital, it may be said that they were not printers in vain.

Because of my fondness for newspapers and magazines, it is a grief to me that the Spanish press should be so weak, so poor, so pusillanimous and stiff-jointed.

Of late, while the foreign press has been expanding and widening its scope, ours has been standing still.

There is, of course, an economic explanation to justify our deficiency, but this is valid only in the matter of quantity, and not as to quality. Comparing our press with that of the rest of the world, a rosary of negation might easily be made up in this fashion:

Our press does not concern itself with what is of universal interest.

Our press does not concern itself with what is of national interest.

Our press does not concern itself with literature.

Our press does not concern itself with philosophy.

And so on to infinity.

Corpus Barga has told me that when Señor Groizard, a relative of his, was ambassador to the Vatican, Leo XIII once inquired of him, in a jargon of Italo-Spanish, in the presence of the papal secretary, Cardinal Rampolla:

"Does the Señor Ambasciatore speak Italian?"

"No, not Italian, although I understand it a little."

"Does the Señor Ambasciatore speak English?"

"No, not English, I do not speak that," replied Groizard.

"Does the Señor Ambasciatore speak German?"

"No German, no Dutch; not at all."

"No doubt then the Señor Ambasciatore speaks French?"

"French? No. I am able to translate it a little, but I do not speak it."

"Then what does the Señor Ambasciatore speak?" asked Leo XIII, smiling that Voltairian smile of his at his secretary.

"Then Señor Ambasciatore speaks a heavy back-country dialect called Extramaduran," replied Rampolla del Tindaro, bending over to His Holiness's ear.

The Spanish press has made a resolution, now of long standing, to speak nothing but a back-country dialect called Extramaduran.

Our Journalists

Our journalists supply the measure of our journals. When the great names are those of Miguel Moya, Romeo, Rocamora and Don Pío, what are we to think of the little fellows?

Speaking generally, the Spanish journalist is interested in politics, in theatres, in bull fights, and in nothing else; whatever is beyond these, does not concern him. Not even the *feuilleton* attracts his attention. A wooden, highly mannered phrase sponsored by Maura, is much more stimulating to his mind than the most sensational piece of news.

The Spanish newspaper man is endowed with an extraordinary lack of imagination and of curiosity. I recall having given a friend, who was a journalist, a little book of Nietzsche's to read, which he returned with the remark that he had not been able to get through it, as it was insufferable drivel. I have heard the same opinion, or similar ones, expressed by journalists of Ibsen, Schopenhauer, Dostoievsky, Stendhal and all the most stimulating minds of Europe.

The wretched Saint Aubin, wretched certainly as a critic, used to ridicule Tolstoi and the illness which resulted in his death, maintaining that it was nothing more than an advertisement. The most benighted vulgarity reigns in our press.

Upon occasion, vulgarity goes hand in hand with an ignorance which is astounding. I remember going to a café on the Calle de Alcalá known as la Maison Dorée one afternoon with Regoyos. Felipe Trigo, the novelist, sat down at our table with a friend of his, a journalist, I believe, from America. I have never been a friend of Trigo's, and could never take any interest either in the man or his work, which to my mind is tiresome and commercially erotic, besides being absolutely devoid of all charm.

Regoyos, who is effusive by nature, soon became engaged in conversation with them, and the talk turned upon artistic subjects, in which he was interested, and then to his travels abroad.

Trigo put in his oar and uttered a number of preposterous statements. In particular, he described a ship which had unloaded at Milan. When Regoyos pointed out that Milan was not a seaport, he replied:

"Probably it was some other place then. What is the difference?"

He continued with a string of geographical and anthropological blunders, which were concurred in by the journalist, while Regoyos and I sat by in amazement.

When we left the café, Regoyos inquired:

"Could they have been joking?"

"No; nonsense. They do not believe that such things are worth knowing. They think they are petty details which might be useful to railway porters. Trigo imagines that he is a magician, who understands the female mind."

"Well, does he?" asked Regoyos, with naïve innocence.

"How can he understand anything? The poor fellow is ignorant. His other attainments are on a par with his geography."

The ignorance of authors and journalists is accompanied as a matter of course by a total want of comprehension. A number of years ago, a rich young man called at my house, intending to found a review. During the conversation, he explained that he was a Murcian, a lawyer and a follower of Maura.

Finally, after expounding his literary ideas, he informed me that Ricardo León, who at that time had just published his first novel, would, in his opinion, come to be acknowledged as the first novelist of Europe. He also assured me that Dickens's humour was absolutely vulgar, cheap and out of date.

"I am not surprised that you should think so," I said to him. "You are from Murcia, you are a lawyer and a Maurista; naturally, you like Ricardo León, and it is equally natural that you should not like Dickens."

Persons who imagine that it is of no consequence whether Milan is a seaport or not, who believe that Nietzsche is a drivelling ass, and who make bold to tell us that Dickens is a cheap author—in one word, young gentlemen lawyers who are partisans of Maura, are the people who provide copy for our press. How can the Spanish press be expected to be different from what it is?

AMERICANS

Unquestionably, Spaniards suffer much from the uncertainty of information and narrowness of view inevitable to those who live apart from the main currents of life.

In comparison with the English, the Germans, or the French, whether we like it or not, we appear provincial. We are provincials who possess more or less talent, but nevertheless we are provincials.

So it is that an Italian, a Russian, or a Swede prefers to read a book by a mediocre Parisian, such as Marcel Prévost, to one by a writer of genuine talent, such as Galdós; it also explains why the canvases of second rate painters such as David, Gericault, or Ingres are more highly esteemed in the market than those of a painter of genius like Goya.

To be provincial has its virtues as well as its defects. At times the provincial are accompanied by universal elements, which blend and form a masterpiece. This was the case with *Don Quixote*, with the etchings of Goya and the dramas of Ibsen. Similarly, among new peoples, provincial stupidity will often form a blend with an obtuseness which is world-wide. The aridness and infertility characteristic of the soil combine with the detritus of fashion and the follies of the four quarters of the globe. The result is a child-like type, petulant, devoid of virtue, and utterly destitute of a single manly quality. This is the American type. America is *par excellence* the continent of stupidity.

The American has not yet outgrown the monkey in him and remains in the imitative stage.

I have no particular reason to dislike Americans. My hostility towards them arises merely from the fact that I have never known one who had the air of being anybody, who impressed me as a man.

You frequently meet a man in the interior of Spain, in some small village, perhaps, whose conversation conveys the impression that he is a real man, wrought out of the ore that is most human and most noble. At such times one becomes reconciled to one's country, for all its charlatans and hordes of sharpers.

An American never appears to be calm, serene and collected. There are plenty who seem to be wild, impulsive creatures, driven on by sanguinary fury, while others disclose the vanity of the chorus girl, or a self-conceit which is wholly ridiculous.

My lack of sympathy for Spanish-Americans extends to their literary productions. Everything that I have read by South Americans, and I bear in mind the not disinterested encomiums of Unamuno, I have found to be both poor and deficient in substance.

Beginning with Sarmiento's *Facundo*, which is heavy, cheap, and uninteresting, and coming down to the latest productions of Ingenieros, Manuel Ugarte, Ricardo Rojas and Contreras, this is true without exception.

What a deluge of shoddy snobbery and vulgar display pours out of America!

It is often argued that Spaniards should eulogize South Americans for political reasons. This is one of many recommendations which proceed from the craniums of gentlemen who top themselves off with silk hats and who carry a lecture inside which is in demand by Ibero-American societies.

I have no faith that this brand of politics will be productive of results.

Citizens of old, civilized countries are still sensible to flattery and compliment, but what are you to tell an Argentine who is fully convinced that Argentina is a more important country than England or Germany, because she raises a large quantity of wheat, to say nothing of a great number of cows?

Whenever Unamuno writes he decries Kant, Schopenhauer and Nietzsche, and then promptly eulogizes the mighty General Aníbal Pérez and the great poet Diocleciano Sánchez, who hail from the pampas. To these fellows, such praise seems grudging enough. Salvador Rueda himself must appear tame to these hide-stretchers.

XVI

POLITICS

I have always been a liberal radical, an individualist and an anarchist. In the first place, I am an enemy of the Church; in the second place, I am an enemy of the State. When these great powers are in conflict I am a partisan of the State as against the Church, but on the day of the State's triumph, I shall become an enemy of the State. If I had lived during the French Revolution, I should have been an internationalist of the school of Anacarsis Clootz; during the struggle for liberty, I should have been one of the *Carbonieri*.

To the extent in which liberalism has been a destructive force, inimical to the past, it enthralls me. The fight against religious prejudice and the aristocracy, the suppression of religious communities, inheritance taxes—in short, whatever has a tendency to pulverize completely the ancient order of society, fills me with a great joy. On the other hand, insofar as liberalism is constructive, as it has been for example in its advocacy of universal suffrage, in its democracy, and in its system of parliamentary government, I consider it ridiculous and valueless as well.

Even today, wherever it is obliged to take the aggressive, it seems to me that the good in liberalism is not exhausted; but wherever it has become an accomplished fact, and is accepted as such, it neither interests me nor enlists my admiration.

VOTES AND APPLAUSE

In our present day democracy, there are only two effective sanctions: votes and applause.

Those are all. Just as in the old days men committed all sorts of crimes in order to please their sovereign, now they commit similar crimes in order to satisfy the people.

And this truth has been recognized from Aristotle to Burke.

Democracy ends in histrionism.

A man who gets up to talk before a crowd must of necessity be an actor. I have wondered from time to time if I might not have certain histrionic gifts myself; however, when I have put them to the test, I have found that they were not sufficient. I have made six or seven speeches during my brief political career. I spoke in Valencia, in a pelota court, and I delivered an address at Barcelona in the Casa del Pueblo, in both of which places I was applauded generously. Nevertheless the applause failed to intoxicate me; it produced no impression upon me whatever. It seemed too much like mere noise—noise made by men's hands, and having nothing to do with myself.

I am not good enough as an actor to be a politician.

POLITICIANS

I have never been able to feel any enthusiasm for Spanish politicians. We hear a great deal about Cánovas. Cánovas has always impressed me as being as bad an orator as he was a writer. When I first read his *Bell of Huesca*, I could not contain myself for laughing. As far as his speeches are concerned, I have also read a few, and find them horribly heavy, diffuse, monotonous and deficient in style. I hear that Cánovas is a great historian, but if so, I am not acquainted with that side of him.

Castelar was unquestionably a man of exceptional gifts as a writer, but he failed to take advantage of them, and they were utterly dissipated. He lacked what most Spaniards of the 19th Century lacked with him; that is, reserve.

When Echegaray was made Minister of Finance, he was already an old man. A reporter called one day to interview him at the Ministry, and Echegaray confessed that he was without any very clear idea as to just what the duties of his office were to be. When the reporter took leave of the dramatist, he remarked:

"Don José, you are not going to be comfortable here; it is cold in the building. Besides, the air is too fresh."

Echegaray replied:

"Yes, and your description suits me exactly."

This cynically cheap joke might have fallen appropriately from the tongues of the majority of Spanish politicians. Among these male *bailarinas*, nearly all of whom date back to the Revolution of September, we may find, indeed, some men of austere character: Salmerón, Pí y Margall and Costa. Salmerón was an inimitable actor, but an actor who was sincere in his part. He was the most marvellous orator that I have ever heard.

As a philosopher, he was of no account, and as a politician he was a calamity.

Pí y Margall, whom I met once in his own home where I went in company with Azorín, was no more a politician or a philosopher than was Salmerón. He was a journalist, a popularizer of other men's ideas, gifted with a style at once clear and concise. Pí y Margall was sincere, enamoured of ideas, and took but little thought of himself.

As to Costa, I confess that he was always antipathetic to me. Like Nakens, he was a man who lived upon the estimation in which he was held by others, pretending all the while that he attached no importance to it whatever. Aguirre Metaca once told me that while he was connected with a paper in Saragossa, he had solicited an interview with Costa, and thereupon Costa wrote the interview himself, referring to himself here and there in it as the

Lion of Graus. I cannot accept Costa as a modern European, intellectually. He was a figure for the Cortes of Cadiz, solemn, pompous, becollared and rhetorical. He was one of those actors who abound in southern countries, who are laid to rest in their graves without ever having had the least idea that their entire lives have been nothing but stage spectacles.

REVOLUTIONISTS

Whether politicians or authors, the Spanish revolutionists always smack to my mind of the property room, and especially is this true of the authors. Zozaya, Morote and Dicenta have passed for many years now as terrible men, both destructive and great innovators. But how ridiculous! Zozaya, like Dicenta, has never done anything but manipulate the commonplace, failing to impart either lightness or novelty to it, as have Valera and Anatole France, succeeding only on the other hand in making it more plumbeous and indigestible.

Speaking of Luis Morote, against whom I urge nothing as a man, he has always been a bugbear to me, the personification of dullness, of vulgarity, of everything that lacks interest and charm. I can conceive nothing lower than an article by Morote.

"What talent that man has! What a revolutionary personality!" they used to say in Valencia, and once the janitor at the Club added: "To think I knew that man when he was only this high!" And he held out his hand about a metre above the ground.

Spain has never produced any revolutionists. Don Nicolás Estévanez, who imagined himself an anarchist, would fly into a rage if he read an article which concealed a gallicism in it.

"Do not bother your head about gallicisms," I used to say to him. "What do they matter, anyway?"

No, we have never had any revolutionists in Spain. That is, we have had only one: Ferrer.

He was certainly not a man of great mind. When he talked, he was on the level of Morote and Zozaya, which is nothing more nor less than the level of everybody else; but when it came to action, he did amount to something, and that something was dangerous.

LERROUX

My only experience in politics was gained with Lerroux.

One Sunday, seven or eight years ago, on coming out of my house and crossing the Plaza de San Marcial, I observed that a great crowd had gathered.

"What is the matter?" I asked.

"Lerroux is coming," they told me.

I delayed a moment and happened on Villar, the composer, among the crowd. We fell to talking of Lerroux and what he might accomplish. A procession was soon formed, which we followed, and we found ourselves in front of the editorial offices of *El Pais*.

"Shall we go in?" asked Villar. "Do you know Lerroux?"

I had met Lerroux in the days when *El Progreso* was still published, having called once with Maeztu at his office; afterwards I saw him in Barcelona in a large shed, which, if I recall rightly, went by the name of "La Fraternidad Republicana," and then I was accompanied by Azorín and Junoy.

Villar and I went upstairs and greeted Lerroux in the offices of *El Pais*.

"Estévanez has spoken of you to me," he said. "Is he well?"

"Yes, very well."

A few days later, Lerroux invited me to dinner at the Café Inglés. Lerroux, Fuente and I dined together, and then fell to talking. Lerroux asked me to join his party, whereupon I pointed out the qualifications which were lacking in me, which were necessary to a politician. Shortly after, I was nominated as a candidate for the City Council, and I addressed a number of meetings, although always coldly, and never at high tension.

While I was with Lerroux, I was never treated save with consideration.

Why did I leave his party? Chiefly because of differences as to ideas and as to tactics. Lerroux wished to organize his party into a party of law and order, so that it might be capable of governing, and also to have it friendly with the Army. I was of the opinion that it ought to be a revolutionary party, not in the sense that I was thinking of erecting barricades, but I wished it to contest, to upset things, and to protest against injustice.

What Lerroux wanted was a party of orators who could speak at public meetings, a party of office-holders, councillors, provincial deputies and the like, while I held, and still hold, that the only efficacious revolutionary weapon is the printed page. Lerroux was anxious to transform the radical party into something aristocratic and Castilian; I desired to see it retain its Catalan character, and continue to wear blouses and rope-soled shoes.

I withdrew from the party for these reasons, to which I may add Lerroux's attitude of indifference upon the occasion of the execution of the stoker of the "Numancia."

Not many months after, I met him on the Carrera de San Jerónimo, and he said to me:

"I have read your diatribes."

"They were not directed against you, but against your politics. I shall never speak ill of you, because I have no cause."

"Yes," he replied, "I know that at heart you are one of my friends."

AN OFFER

A number of years ago, when the Conservatives were in power and Dato was President of the Ministry, Azorín brought me word that Sánchez Guerra, then Minister of the Interior, wished to see me and to have a little talk, as perhaps some way might be arranged by which I might be made deputy. During the afternoon, I accompanied Azorín to the Ministry, and we saw the Minister.

He informed me that he would like to have me enter the Congress.

"I should like to myself," I replied, "but it would appear to me rather difficult."

"But is there not some town where you are well known, and where you have influence?"

"No, none whatever."

"How would you like then to be deputy to represent the Government?"

"As a regular?"

"Yes."

"As a Conservative?"

"Yes."

I thought a moment and said: "No, I can never be a Conservative, however it might suit my interest to be so. Try as hard as I might, I should never succeed."

"That is the only way in which we can make you deputy."

"Well, it cannot be helped! I must resign myself then to amount to nothing."

Thanking the Minister for his kindness. Azorín and I walked out of the Ministry of the Interior.

SOCIALISTS

As for Socialists, I have never cared to have anything to do with them. One of the most offensive things about Socialists, which is more offensive than their pedantry, than their charlatanry, than their hypocrisy, is their inquisitorial instinct for prying into other people's lives. Whether Pablo Iglesias travels first or third class, has been for years one of the principal topics of dispute between Socialists and their opponents.

Fifteen years ago I was in Tangier, where I had been sent by the *Globo*, and, upon my return, a newspaper man who had socialistic ideas, reproached me:

"You talk a great deal about the working man, but I see you were living in the best hotel in Tangier."

I answered: "In the first place, I have never spoken of the workingman with any fervour. Furthermore, I am not such a slave as to be too cowardly to take what life offers as it comes, as you are. I take what I can that I want, and when I do not take it, it is because I cannot get it."

LOVE OF THE WORKINGMAN

To gush over the workingman is one of the commonplaces of the day which is utterly false and hypocritical. Just as in the 18th century sympathy was with the simple hearted citizen, so today we talk about the workingman. The term workingman can never be anything but a grammatical common denominator. Among workingmen, as among the bourgeoisie, there are all sorts of people. It is perfectly true that there are certain characteristics, certain defects, which may be exaggerated in a given class, because of its special environment and culture. The difference in Spanish cities between the labouring man and the bourgeoisie is not very great. We frequently see the workingman leap the barrier into the bourgeoisie, and then disclose himself as a unique flower of knavery, extortion and misdirected ingenuity. Deep down in the hearts of our revolutionists, I do not believe that there is any real enthusiasm for the workingman.

When the bookshop of Fernando Fé was still fin the Carrera de San Jerónimo, I once heard Blasco Ibáñez say with the cheapness that is his distinguishing trait, laughing meanwhile ostentatiously, that a republic in Spain would mean the rule of shoemakers and of the scum of the streets.

THE CONVENTIONALIST BARRIOVERO

Barriovero, a conventionalist, according to Grandmontagne—yes, and how keen the scent of this American for such matters!—attended the opening of a radical club in the Calle del Príncipe with a party of friends. We were all drinking champagne. Like other revolutionists and parvenus generally, Lerroux is a victim of the superstition of champagne.

"Aha, suppose those workingmen should see us drinking champagne!" suggested some one.

"What of it?" asked another.

"I only wish for my part," Barriovero interrupted with a show of sentiment, "that the workingman could learn to drink champagne."

"Learn to drink it?" I burst out, "I see no difficulty about that. He could drink champagne as well as anything else."

"Not at all," said Barriovero the conventionalist, very gravely. "He has the superstition of the peasant; he thinks he must leave enough wine to cover the bottom of the glass."

I doubt whether this observation will attract the attention of any future Plutarch, although it might very well do so, as it expresses most I clearly the distinction which exists in the minds of our revolutionists between the workingman and the young gentleman.

ANARCHISTS

I have had a number of acquaintances among anarchists. Some of them are dead; the majority of the others have changed their ideas. It is apparent nowadays that the anarchism of Reclus and Kropotkin is out of date, and entirely a thing of the past. The same tendencies will reappear under other forms, and present new aspects. Among anarchists, I have known Elysée Reclus, whom I met in the editorial offices of a publication called *L'Humanité Nouvelle*, which was issued in Paris in the Rue des Saints-Pères. I have also met Sebastien Faure during a mass meeting organized in the interests of one Guerin, who had taken refuge in a house in the Rue de Chabrol some eighteen or twenty years ago. I have had relations with Malatesta and Tarrida del Marmol. As a matter of fact, both these anarchists escorted me one afternoon from Islington, where Malatesta lived, to the door of the St. James Club, one of the most aristocratic retreats in London, where I had an appointment to meet a diplomat.

As for active anarchists, I have known a number, two or three of whom have been dynamiters.

THE MORALITY OF THE ALTERNATING PARTY SYSTEM

The only difference between the morality of the Liberal party and that of the Conservative party is one of clothes. Among Conservatives the most primitive clout seems to be slightly more ample, but not noticeably so.

The preoccupations of both are purely with matters of style. The only distinction is that the Conservatives make off with a great deal at once, while the Liberals take less, but do it often.

This is in harmony with the law of mechanics according to which what is gained in force is lost in velocity and what is gained in intensity is lost in expansion. After all, no doubt morality in politics should be a negligible quantity. Honest, upright men who hearken only to the voice of conscience, never get on in politics, neither are they ever practical, nor good for anything.

To succeed in politics, a certain facility is necessary, to which must be added ambition and a thirst for glory. The last is the most innocent of the three.

ON OBEYING THE LAW

It is safe, it seems to me, to assume the following axioms: First, to obey the law is in no sense to attain justice; second, it is not possible to obey the law strictly, thoroughly, in any country in the world.

That obeying the law has nothing to do with justice is indisputable, and this is especially true in the political sphere, in which it is easy to point to a rebel, such as Martínez Campos, who has been elevated to the plane of a great man and who has been immortalized by a statue upon his death, and then to a rebel such as Sánchez Moya, who Was merely shot. The only difference between the men was in the results attained, and in the manner of their exit.

Hence I say that Lerroux was not only base, but obtuse and absurdly wanting in human feeling and revolutionary sympathy, when he concurred in the execution of the stoker of the "Numancia."

If law and justice are identical and to comply with the law is invariably to do justice, then what can be the distinction between the progressive and the conservative? On the other hand, the revolutionist has no alternative but to hold that law and justice are not the same, and so he is obliged to subscribe to the benevolent character of all crimes which are altruistic and social in their purposes, whether they are reactionary or anarchistic in tendency.

Now the second axiom, which is to the effect that there is no city or country in the world in which it is possible to obey the law thoroughly, is also self-evident. A certain class of common crimes, such as robbery, cheating and swindling, murder and the like, are followed by a species of automatic punishment in all quarters of the civilized world, in spite of exceptions in specific cases, which result from the intervention of political bosses and similar influences; but there are other offenses which meet with no such automatic punishment. In these pardon and penalty are meted out in a spirit of pure opportunism.

I was discussing Zurdo Olivares one day with Emiliano Iglesias in the office of *El Radical*, when I asked him:

"How was it that Zurdo Olivares could save himself after playing such an active role in the tragic week at Barcelona?"

"Zurdo's salvation was indirectly owing to me," replied Iglesias.

"But, my dear sir!"

"Yes, indeed."

"How did that happen?"

"Very naturally. There were three cases to be tried; one was against Ferrer, one against Zurdo, and another against me. A friend who enjoyed the necessary influence, succeeded in quashing the case against me, as a matter of personal favour, and as it seemed rather barefaced to make an exception alone in my favour, it was decided to include Zurdo Olivares, who, thanks to the arrangement, escaped being shot."

"Then, if an influential friend of yours had not been a member of the Ministry, you would both have been shot in the moat at Montjuich?"

"Beyond question."

And this took place in the heyday of Conservative power.

THE STERNNESS OF THE LAW

There are men who believe that the State, as at present constituted, is the end and culmination of all human effort. According to this view, the State is the best possible state, and its organization is considered so perfect that its laws, discipline and formulae are held to be sacred and immutable in men's eyes. Maura and all conservatives must be reckoned in this group, and Lerroux too, appears to belong with them, as he holds discipline in such exalted respect.

On the other hand, there are persons who believe that the entire legal structure is only a temporary scaffolding, and that what is called justice today may be thought savagery tomorrow, so that it is the part of wisdom not to look so much to the rule of the present as to the illumination of the future.

Since it is impossible to effect in practice automatic enforcement of the law, especially in the sphere of political crimes, because of the unlimited power of pardon vested in the hands of our public men, it would seem judicious to err upon the side of mercy rather than upon that of severity. Better fail the law and pardon a repulsive, bloody beast such as Chato de Cuqueta, than shoot an addle-headed unfortunate such as Clemente García, or a dreamer like Sánchez Moya, whose hands were innocent of blood.

It was pointed out a long time ago that laws are like cobwebs; they catch the little flies, and let the big ones pass through.

How very severe, how very determined our politicians are with the little flies, but how extremely affable they are with the big ones!

XVII

MILITARY GLORY

No, I have not made up my mind upon the issues of this war. If it were possible to determine what is best for Europe, I should of course desire it, but this I do not know, and so I am uncertain. I am preoccupied by the consequences which may follow the war in Spain. Some believe that there will be an increase of militarism, but I doubt it.

Many suppose that the crash of the present war will cause the prestige of the soldier to mount upward like the spray, so that we shall have nothing but uniforms and clanking of spurs throughout the world very shortly, while the sole topics of conversation will be mortars, batteries and guns.

In my judgment those who take this standpoint are mistaken. The present conflict will not establish war in higher favour.

Perhaps its glories may not be diminished utterly. It may be that man must of necessity kill, burn, and trample under foot, and that these excesses of brutality are symptoms of collective health.

Even if this be so, we may be sure that military glory is upon the eve of an eclipse.

Its decline began when the professional armies became nothing more than armed militia, and from the moment that it became apparent that a soldier might be improvised from a countryman with marvellous rapidity.

THE OLD-TIME SOLDIER

Formerly, a soldier was a man of daring and adventure, brave and audacious, preferring an irregular life to the narrowing restraints of civil existence.

The old time soldier trusted in his star without scruple and without fear, and imagined that he could dominate fate as the gambler fancies that he masters the laws of chance.

Valour, recklessness, together with a certain rough eloquence, a certain itch to command, lay at the foundation of his life. His inducements were pay, booty, showy uniforms and splendid horses. The soldier's life was filled with adventure, he conquered wealth, he conquered women, and he roamed through unknown lands.

Until a few years ago, the soldier might have been summed up in three words: he was brave, ignorant and adventurous.

The warrior of this school passed out of Europe about the middle of the 19th Century. He became extinct in Spain at the conclusion of our Second Civil War.

Since that day there has been a fundamental change in the life of the soldier.

War has taken on greater magnitude, while the soldier has become more refined, and it is not to be denied that both war and the fighting man are losing their traditional prestige.

DOWN GOES PRESTIGE

The causes of this diminution of prestige are various. Some are moral, such as the increased respect for human life, and the disfavour with which the more aggressive, crueler qualities have come to be regarded. Others, however, and perhaps these are of more importance, are purely esthetic. Through a combination of circumstances, modern warfare, although more tragic than was ancient warfare, and even more deadly, nevertheless has been deprived of its spectacular features.

Capacity for esthetic appreciation has its limits. Nobody is able to visualize a battle in which two million men are engaged; it can only be imagined as a series of smaller battles. In one of these modern battles, substantially all the traditional elements which we have come to associate with war, have disappeared. The horse, which bulks so largely in the picture of a battle as it presents itself to our minds, scarcely retains any importance at all; for the most part, automobiles, bicycles and motor cycles have taken its place. These contrivances may be useful, but they do not make the same appeal to the popular imagination.

SCIENCE AND THE PICTURESQUE

Upon taking over warfare, science stripped it of its picturesqueness. The commanding general no longer cavorts upon his charger, nor smiles as the bullets whistle about him, while he stands surrounded by an ornamental general staff, whose breasts are covered with ribbons and medals representing every known variety of hardware, whether monarchical or republican.

Today the general sits in a room, surrounded by telephones and telegraph apparatus. If he smiles at all, it is only before the camera.

An officer scarcely ever uses a sword, nor does he strut about adorned with all his crosses and medals, nor does he wear the resplendent uniforms of other days. On the contrary, his uniform is ugly and dirt coloured, and innocent of devices.

This officer is without initiative, he is subordinated to a fixed general plan; surprises on either one side or the other, are almost out of the question.

The plan of battle is rigid and detailed. It permits neither originality nor display of individuality upon the part of the generals, the lesser officers, or the private soldiers. The individual is swallowed up by the collective force. Outstanding types do not occur; nobody develops the marked personality of the generals of the old school.

Besides this, individual bravery, when not reinforced by other qualities, is of less and less consequence. The bold, adventurous youth who, years ago, would have been an embryo Murat, Messina, Espartero or Prim, would be rejected today to make room for a mechanic who had the skill to operate a machine, or for an aviator or an engineer who might be capable of solving in a crisis a problem of pressing danger.

The prestige of the soldier, even upon the battle field, has fallen today below that of the man of science.

WHAT WE NEED TODAY

There are still some persons of a romantic turn of mind who imagine that none but the soldier who defends his native land, the priest who appeases the divine wrath and at the same time inculcates the moral law, and the poet who celebrates the glories of the community, are worthy to be leaders of the people.

But the man of the present age does not desire any leaders.

He has found that when someone wears red trousers or a black cassock, or is able to write shorter lines than himself, it is no indication that he is any better, nor any braver, nor any more moral, nor capable of deeper feeling than he.

The man of today will have no magicians, no high priests and no mysteries. He is capable of being his own priest, his own soldier when it is necessary, and of fighting for himself; he requires no specialists in courage, in morals, nor in the realm of sentiment and feeling. What we need today are good men and wise men.

OUR ARMIES

Prussian militarism has been explained upon the theory that it was a development consequent upon a realization of the benefits which had accrued to Prussia through war. As a matter of fact, however, it is not possible to explain all militarism in this way. Certainly in Spain neither wars nor the army have been of the slightest benefit to the country.

If we consider the epoch which goes by the name of contemporary history, that is to say from the French Revolution to the present time, we shall perceive immediately that we have not been over fortunate.

The French Republic declared war upon us in 1793. A campaign of astuteness, a tactical warfare was waged by us upon the frontiers, upon occasion not without success, until finally the French army grew strong enough to sweep us back, and to cross the Ebro.

We took part in the battle of Trafalgar in 1805. Spain presented a fine appearance, she made a mighty gesture with her Gravinas, her Churrucas and her Alavas, but the battle itself was a disaster.

In 1808 the War of Independence broke out, providing another splendid exhibition of popular fervour. In this war, the regular Army was the force which accomplished least. The war took its character from the guerrillas, from the dwellers in the towns. The campaign was directed by Englishmen. The Spanish army suffered more defeats than it won victories, while its administrative and technical organization was deplorable. The intervention of Angoulême followed in 1823. The Army was composed of liberal officers, but it contained no troops, so that all they ever did was to retire before the enemy, as he was more numerous and more powerful.

The Spanish cause in America was hopeless before the fighting began. The land was enormous, troops were few, and in large measure composed of Indians. What the English were never able to do in the fulness of their power, was not to be accomplished by Spaniards in their decadence. Our First Civil War, which was fierce, terrible, and waged without quarter, called into being a valorous liberal army, and soldiers sprang up of the calibre of Espartero, Zurbano and Narváez, but simultaneously a powerful Carlist army was organized under leaders of military genius, such as Zumalacárregui and Cabrera. Victory for either side was impossible, and the war ended in compromise.

The Second Civil War also resulted in a system of pacts and compromises far more secret than the Convention of Vergara. The Cuban war and the war in the Philippines, as afterwards the war with the United States, were calamitous, while the present campaign in Morocco has not one redeeming feature.

From the War of the French Revolution to this very day, the African War has been the only one in which our forces have met with the slightest success.

Nevertheless, our soldiers aspire to a position of dominance in the country equal to that attained by the French soldiers subsequent to Jena, and by the Germans after Sedan.

A WORD FROM KUROKI, THE JAPANESE

"Gentlemen," said General Kuroki, speaking at a banquet tendered to him in New York, "I cannot aspire to the applause of the world, because I have created nothing, I have invented nothing. I am only a soldier."

If these are not his identical words, they convey the meaning of them.

This victorious, square-headed Mongolian had gotten into his head what the dolichocephalic German blond, who, according to German anthropologists is the highest product of Europe, and the brachycephalic brunette of Gaul and the Latin and the Slav have never been able to understand.

Will they ever be able to understand it? Perhaps they never will be able.

EPILOGUE

When I sat down to begin these pages, somewhat at random, my intention was to write an autobiography, accompanying it with such comments as might suggest themselves. Looking continually to the right and to the left, I have lost my way, and this book is the result.

I have not attempted to correct or embellish it. So many books, trimmed up nicely and well-padded, go to their graves every year to be forgotten forever, that it has hardly seemed worth while to bedeck this one. I am not a believer in *maquillage* for the dead.

Now one word more as to the subject of the book, which is I.

If I were to live two hundred years at the very least, I might be able to realize, by degrees, the maximum programme which I have laid down for my life. As it scarcely seems possible that a man could live to such an age, which is attained only by parrots, I find myself with no alternative but to limit myself to a small portion of the introductory section of my minimum programme, and this, as a matter of fact, I am content to do.

With hardship and effort, and the scanty means at my command, I have succeeded in acquiring a house and garden in my own country, a comfortable retreat which is sufficient for my needs. I have gathered a small library in the house, which I hope will grow with time, besides a few manuscripts and some curious prints. I do not believe that I have ever harmed any man deliberately, so my conscience does not trouble me. If my ideas are fragmentary and ill-considered, I have done my best to make them sound, clear, and complete, so that it is not my fault if they are not so.

I have become independent financially. I not only support myself, but I am able to travel occasionally upon the proceeds of my pen.

A Russian publishing house, another in Germany, and another in the United States are bringing out my books, paying me, moreover, for the right of translation; and I am satisfied. I have friends of both sexes in Madrid and in the Basque provinces, who seem already like old friends, because I have grown fond of them. As I face old age, I feel that I am walking upon firmer ground than I did in my youth.

In a short time, what a few years ago the sociologists used to call involution—that is, a turning in—will begin to take place in my brain; the cranial sutures will become petrified, and an automatic limitation of the mental horizon will soon come.

I shall accept involution, petrification of the sutures and limitation with good grace. I have never rebelled against logic, nor against nature, against the lightning or the thunder storm. No sooner does one gain the crest of the hill of life than at once he begins to descend rapidly. We know a great deal the moment that we realize that nobody knows anything. I am a little melancholy now and a little rheumatic; it is time to take salicylates and to go out and work in the garden—a time for meditation and for long stories, for watching the flames as they flare upward under the chimney piece upon the hearth.

I commend myself to the event. It is dark outside, but the door of my house stands open. Whoever will, be he life or be he death, let him come in.

PALINODE AND FRESH OUTBURST OF IRE

A few days ago I left the house with the manuscript of this book, to which I have given the name of *Youth and Egolatry*, on my way to the post office.

It was a romantic September morning, swathed in thick, white mist. A blue haze of thin smoke rose upward from the shadowy houses of the neighbouring settlement, vanishing in the mist. Meanwhile, the birds were singing, and a rivulet close by murmured in the stillness.

Under the influence of the homely, placid country air, I felt my spirit soften and grow more humble, and I began to think that the manuscript which I carried in my hand was nothing more than a farrago of foolishness and vulgarity.

The voice of prudence, which was also that of cowardice, cautioned me:

"What is the good of publishing this? Will it bring you reputation?"

"Certainly not."

"Have you anything to gain by it?"

"Probably not either."

"Then, why irritate and offend this one and that by saying things which, after all, are nobody's business?"

To the voice of prudence, however, my habitual self replied:

"But what you have written is sincere, is it not? What do you care, then, what they think about it?"

But the voice of prudence continued:

"How quiet everything is about you, how peaceful! This is life, after all, and the rest is madness, vanity and vain endeavour."

There was a moment when I was upon the point of tossing my manuscript into the air, and I believe I should have done so, could I have been sure that it would have dematerialized itself immediately like smoke; or I would have thrown it into the river, if I had felt certain that the current would have swept it out to sea.

* * * * *

This afternoon I went to San Sebastian to buy paper and salicylate of soda, which is less agreeable.

A number of public guards were riding together in the car on the way over, along the frontier. They were discussing bull fighters, El Gallo and Belmonte, and also the disorders of the past few days.

"Too bad that Maura and La Cierva are not in power," said one of them, who was from Murcia, smiling and exhibiting his decayed teeth. "They would have made short work of this."

"They are in reserve for the finish," said another, with, the solemnity of a pious scamp.

Returning from San Sebastian, I happened on a family from Madrid in the same car. The father was weak, jaundiced and sour-visaged; the mother was a fat brunette, with black eyes, who was loaded down with jewels, while her face was made up until it was brilliant white, in colour like a stearin candle. A rather good looking daughter of between fifteen and twenty was escorted by a lieutenant who apparently was engaged to her. Finally, there was another girl, between twelve and fourteen, flaccid and lively as a still-life on a dinner table. Suddenly the father, who was reading a newspaper, exclaimed:

"Nothing is going to be done, I can see that; they are already applying to have the revolutionists pardoned. The Government will do nothing."

"I wish they would kill every one of them," broke in the girl who was engaged to the lieutenant. "Think of it! Firing on soldiers! They are bandits."

"Yes, and with such a king as we have!" exclaimed the fat lady, with the paraffine hue, in a mournful tone. "It has ruined our summer. I wish they would shoot every one of them."

"And they are not the only ones," interrupted the father. "The men who are behind them, the writers and leaders, hide themselves, and then they throw the first stones."

Upon entering the house, I found that the final proofs of my book had just arrived from the printer, and sat down to read them.

The words of that family from Madrid still rang in my ears: "I wish they would kill every one of them!"

However one may feel, I thought to myself, it is impossible not to hate such people. Such people are natural enemies. It is inevitable.

Now, reading over the proofs of my book, it seems to me that it is not strident enough. I could wish it were more violent, more anti-middle class.

I no longer hear the voice of prudence seducing me, as it did a few days since, to a palinode in complicity with a romantic morning of white mist.

The zest of combat, of adventure stirs in me again. The sheltered harbour seems a poor refuge in my eyes,—tranquillity and security appear contemptible.

"Here, boy, up, and throw out the sail! Run the red flag of revolution to the masthead of our frail craft, and forth to sea!"

Itzea, September, 1917.

APPENDICES

SPANISH POLITICIANS
ON BAROJA'S ANARCHISTS
NOTE

SPANISH POLITICIANS

The Spanish alternating party system has prevailed as a national institution since the restoration of the monarchy under Alfonso XII. Ostensibly it is based upon manhood suffrage, and in the cities this is the fact, but in the more remote districts the balloting plays but small part in the returns. Upon the dissolution of the Cortes and the resignation of a ministry, one of the two great parties—the liberal party and the conservative party—automatically retires from power, and the other succeeds it, always carrying the ensuing elections by convenient working majorities.

Spain is a poor country. During the half century previous to the restoration of the Bourbons, she was a victim of internecine strife and factional warfare. She is not poor naturally, but her energy has been drawn off; she has been bled white, and needs time to recuperate. The Spaniards are a practical people. They realize this condition. Even the lower classes are tired of fine talking. No people have heard more, and none have profited less by it. The country is not like Russia, a fertile field for the agitator; it looks coldly upon reform. Such response as has been obtained by the radical has come from the labour centres under the stimulus of foreign influences, and more particularly from Barcelona, where the problem is political even before it is an individual one.

For this reason the Spanish Republicans are in large part theorists. The land has been disturbed sufficiently. They would hesitate to inaugurate radical reforms, if power were to be placed in their hands, while the possession of power itself might prove not a little embarrassing. Behind the monarchy lies the republic of 1873, behind Cánovas and Castelar, Pí y Margall; the republic has merged into and was, in a sense, the foundation of the constitutional system of today. Even popular leaders such as Lerroux are quick to recognize this fact, and govern themselves accordingly. The lack of general education today, would render any attempt at the establishment of a thorough-going democracy insecure.

Francisco Ferrer, although idealized abroad, has been no more than a symptom in Spain. Such men even as Angel Guimerá, the dramatist, a Catalan separatist who has been under surveillance for years, or Pere Aldavert, who has suffered imprisonment in Barcelona because of his opinions, while they speak for the proletariat, nevertheless have had scant sympathy for Ferrer's ideas. It would be interesting to know just to what extent these commend themselves to Pablo and Emiliano Iglesias and the professed political Socialists.

Of the existing parties, the Liberal, being more or less an association of groups tending to the left, is the least homogeneous. Its most prominent leader of late years has been the Conde de Romanones, who may scarcely be said to represent a new era. He has shared responsibility with Eduardo Dato.

Among Conservatives, the chief figure has long been Antonio Maura. He is not a young man. Politically, he represents very much what the cordially detested Weyler did in the military sphere. But Maurism today is a very different thing from the Maurism of fifteen years ago, or of the moat of Montjuich. The name of Maura casts a spell over the Conservative imagination. It is the rallying point of innumerable associations of young men of reactionary, aristocratic and clerical tendencies throughout the country, while to progressives it symbolizes the oppressiveness of the old régime.

ON BAROJA'S ANARCHISTS

Baroja's memoirs afford convincing proof of his contact with radicals of all sorts and classes, from stereotyped republicans such as Barriovero, or the Argentine Francisco Grandmontagne, correspondent of *La Prensa* of Buenos Aires, to active anarchists of the type of Mateo Morral.

Morral was an habitué of a cafe in the Calle de Alcalá at Madrid, where Baroja was accustomed to go with his friends to take coffee, and, in the Spanish phrase, to attend his *tertulia*. Morral would listen to these conversations. After his attempt to assassinate the King and Queen in the Calle Mayor on their return from the Royal wedding ceremony, Baroja went to view Morral's body, but was refused admittance. A drawing of Morral was made at the time, however, by Ricardo Baroja.

In this connection, José Nakens, to whom the author pays his compliments on an earlier page, was subjected to an unusual experience. Nakens, who was a sufficiently mild gentleman, had taken a needy radical into his house, and had given him shelter. This personage made a point of inveighing to Nakens continually against Cánovas del Castillo, proposing to make way with him. When the news of the assassination of Cánovas was cried through the city, Nakens knew for the first that his visitor had been in earnest. He was none other than the murderer Angiolillo.

This anecdote became current in Madrid. Years afterwards when the prime minister Canalejas was shot to death, the assassin recalled it to mind, and repaired to the house of Nakens, who saw in dismay for the second time his radical theories put to violent practical proof. The incident proved extremely embarrassing.

The crime of Morral forms the basis of Baroja's novel *La Dama Errante*. He has also dealt with anarchism in *Aurora Roja* (Red Dawn).

The mutiny on the ship "Numancia," referred to in the text, was an incident of the same period of unrest, which was met with severe repressive measures.

NOTE

The Madrid Ateneo is a learned society maintaining a house on the Calle del Prado, in which is installed a private library of unusual excellence. It has been for many years the principal depository of modern books in Spain, and a favourite resort of scholars and research-workers of the capital.